"I Want You To Be My Fiancée."

"What?" Sheri was sure she'd misunderstood, because she knew Tristan wasn't the marrying kind. She thought he'd said…

"I want you to be my fiancée for the time being. Just until the furor of the press dies down."

She felt the blood rush from her face, and she closed her eyes. Of course it would be temporary.

But sitting there, she felt a sense of rightness all the way to her soul, and she knew she'd say yes to his outrageous proposal for one reason. She was going to find a way to make Tristan Sabina fall in love with her.

Dear Reader,

Since I was a little girl I've been in love with all things French. I think it's because my great-grandmother, though Italian, spent a few years in a girls' school in Marseille before coming to America. She spoke French as fluently as Italian. And my grandmother, her youngest child, would sometimes speak to me in French.

During high school I took French as my required language, and I sent letters to my grandmother in French. It was our little thing that only the two of us did. My youngest sister took French, as well, and we used to speak in French when we didn't want our other sister to know what we were saying!

My obsession with French men began when I was working at Walt Disney World in Florida. Before Disneyland Paris opened, they sent three young French men to our office to learn how Disney worked in order to set up the Paris finance office. These men were dreamy. Tall, dark haired and *very* flirtatious. One in particular used to sit on the edge of my desk and talk to me. I can still hear the rhythm of his words, that accent he had whenever he spoke. So Tristan is an amalgam of these men.

Sheri is a lot like me in some ways. She is used to blending into the background. When she finds herself in the spotlight, she struggles to find her footing. But knowing that she has Tristan helps her find her way.

Happy reading!

Katherine

KATHERINE GARBERA

THE WEALTHY FRENCHMAN'S PROPOSITION

Silhouette
Desire

Published by Silhouette Books
America's Publisher of Contemporary Romance

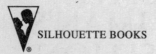
SILHOUETTE BOOKS

ISBN-13: 978-0-373-76851-6
ISBN-10: 0-373-76851-6

THE WEALTHY FRENCHMAN'S PROPOSITION

Copyright © 2008 by Katherine Garbera

Visit Silhouette Books at www.eHarlequin.com

Printed in U.S.A.

Recent books by Katherine Garbera

Silhouette Desire

†*His Wedding-Night Wager* #1708
†*Her High-Stakes Affair* #1714
†*Their Million-Dollar Night* #1720
The Once-a-Mistress Wife #1749
**Make-Believe Mistress* #1798
**Six-Month Mistress* #1802
**High-Society Mistress* #1808
The Greek Tycoon's Secret Heir #1845
The Wealthy Frenchman's Proposition #1851

Silhouette Bombshell

Exposed #10
Night Life #23
The Amazon Strain #43
Exclusive #94

†What Happens in Vegas…
**The Mistresses
*Sons of Privilege

KATHERINE GARBERA

is a strong believer in happily-ever-after. She's written more than thirty-five books and has been nominated for *Romantic Times BOOKreviews* career achievement awards in Series Fantasy and Series Adventure. Her books have appeared on the Waldenbooks/Borders bestseller list for series romance and on the *USA TODAY* extended bestseller list. Visit Katherine on the Web at www.katherinegarbera.com.

This book is dedicated to Rob Elser
who is my knight in shining armor.

Acknowledgments

I have to acknowledge my children Courtney and Lucas who were wonderful while I was writing this book during their summer break. They were extremely understanding in letting me plan events for them around my writing schedule. I know that every mother says she has the best kids in the world—but I really do!

One

"*Bonjour,* Sheri. Did the interoffice pouch arrive yet? I have sent something special in it for you!"

Sheri Donnelly smiled into the phone at Lucille Dumont's greeting. She loved her job at the Sabina Group. She'd been unsure what the future would hold six months earlier, when the small magazine company she worked for had been purchased by the large French conglomerate. But the change was working out beautifully.

Lucille was Sheri's counterpart at the publishing company's Paris office. Though they'd never met, Sheri always pictured Lucille as a chic Parisian. Partly because of the way she sounded over the phone and partly because their boss, publisher Tristan Sabina, had said that Lucille was nothing like her when she'd asked what his other assistant looked like.

"No, why?"

"I sent you the latest copy of *Le Figaro*." Lucille was a devoted reader of all tabloid magazines. She often sent Sheri the French tabloids and loved to receive the gossip rags from the U.S.

"Tristan hates it when you do that."

"He doesn't have to know. And he's on the cover with a gorgeous woman."

"I might be interested in it," Sheri said. Tristan had become kind of an obsession with her. Not anything unhealthy that bordered on stalking, but more of an unquenchable curiosity. She wanted to know all about him. So far, she'd learned that he was demanding but gave praise easily. Plus he was extremely cute. And a widower.

"I thought you would be."

Sheri grimaced. Was she that transparent, even over the phone? "Was there anything else?"

"Yes. I want to know about the woman. She's a

blond American actress, Kate or Jennifer or something. Do you know if he is seeing her?"

An actress? She'd been jealous of the coffee girl from downstairs whom Tristan flirted with every morning. No way could she compete with a beautiful blond actress. Sheri personified plain and dowdy, two things she knew about herself but had never been able to change.

"I don't have any details," Sheri said, smiling at the office mail guy as he dropped off the pouch. Now she was curious to see exactly what was in there.

"See what you can find out when he gets in to the office. You have the inside scoop on this one."

"I'm pretty sure that Tristan will fire me if I start gossiping about his personal life."

"You are right about that." The deep, velvety cadence of Tristan Sabina's voice made her start guiltily.

She gulped and looked up into his steel-gray eyes. "I've got to go, Lucille." She hurriedly said goodbye and hung up the phone, still holding Tristan's gaze.

His thick brown hair was longer in the front than in the back and his face had the healthy glow that came from spending time outdoors and not on a tanning bed. This morning he wore a blue pin-striped shirt, open at the collar, and a tailored navy suit. The sight of him made her want to stare dreamily, which was *so* not like her.

"Talking about me again?"

"Lucille and I have to talk about you," she said, trying for the cheeky tone she usually pulled off easily. "We're your assistants."

"True, but that did not sound like work."

She shrugged, unable to stop her speculative thoughts. Was he dating a Hollywood starlet? And when had it happened?

"What was Lucille calling you about?" he asked as he reached for his messages, and began thumbing through them.

"Oh, you know how she is, always thinking there's something exciting going on here in New York," Sheri said, looking down at her computer screen and hoping he'd just go into his office. She couldn't look at him and not tell him the truth.

"Ms. Donnelly?"

"Hmm...?" she said, still not looking up. Her computer screen was infinitely fascinating at this moment. *Please let him go away.*

"Look at me." She finally did. "What did Lucille ask you about?"

"I told you," she said, dropping her gaze to his open collar.

"Why will you not look me in the eye?" he asked, his accent very pronounced.

"Because I don't want to lie to you."

"Then do not lie to me."

She shrugged again. The last thing she wanted to talk about was his personal life. *Liar.* "It was something she saw in *Le Figaro.*"

"About me and a woman?" he asked.

She nodded.

He didn't say anything else, just stared down at her, and she started to feel really self-conscious. What if, somehow, he could read on her face that she was attracted to him? What if he picked up on that and it made working for him awkward? What if…?

"You have a conference call with Rene in fifteen minutes, and he just sent a lengthy e-mail that you should at least glance at before you talk to him," she said, holding out a copy of the e-mail, which she'd printed out for him.

For a moment she didn't think he was going to let her steer the conversation back to business.

"You are right, of course," he said, taking the papers.

"I highlighted the topics for you and jotted down the information I had on each one."

"Thank you, Ms. Donnelly. I don't know what I would do without you."

She flushed at the compliment. "You're welcome."

She watched until he walked into his office. She was going to kill Lucille. Not that the other woman could have known that Tristan would arrive while they were talking about him, but still....

She reached for the interoffice pouch and opened it. The magazine spilled out. The cover featured Tristan's publicity shot but inset was another picture. The paparazzi hadn't gotten a very good photo, but he looked very amorous, as did the woman wrapped around him. Sheri traced her finger over the line of his eyebrows, ignoring the headline and just concentrating on Tristan.

She was careful never to stare at him at work, that wouldn't be appropriate, but—

"Ms. Donnelly?"

"Yes."

"Put that magazine away."

She blanched and opened her bottom desk drawer, tossing the tabloid in there. "Was there something you wanted?"

"I need the book for the *Global Traveler.*"

"Yes, sir. I think that Maurice has it down the

hall," she said, standing and leaving the office before he could say anything else to her.

Oh, man, this was so not good. Twice in less than ten minutes, he'd caught her slacking on the clock. One of his big no-nos. To be honest, she didn't do a lot of it. But she had a feeling that wasn't going to matter. If she wanted to move up the managerial ladder, perhaps someday become an associate publisher, she'd better not get fired.

She grabbed the book, the big mock-up binder of the issue they were currently working on for their *Global Traveler* magazine, and hurried back to Tristan's office. He was on the speakerphone with his brother, Rene. The conversation was in French and she understood only about every third word they said. Tristan gestured for the book and she handed it to him before leaving the room.

She got back to her desk and saw an instant message from Lucille.

[L.Dumont] Did T walk in while we were talking?
[S.Donnelly] Yes.
[L.Dumont] Did you tell him what we were talking about?

She thought about filling Lucille in but then decided better of it.

[S.Donnelly] I really can't IM right now.
[L.Dumont] OK. Ping me when you can.
[S.Donnelly] Later.

Later, she thought. If she still had a job. She doubted that Tristan would fire her for talking on the phone, especially to Lucille, but she knew he wouldn't hesitate if she gave him enough reason to believe she was more interested in his personal life than in her job.

"Do you need anything else before I go, Mr. Sabina?" Sheri asked right at five o'clock. Not that she had anything really interesting to go home to. But she'd made it a point not to stay late since Tristan had become her boss. She found she liked the office a little too much when only the two of them were still there.

Tristan glanced up from his phone, which he'd been staring at in...amazement? His bangs fell over his forehead, making him look devilishly handsome.

He looked at her assessingly, making her

more nervous. "Actually I do have one more thing to discuss with you, something that has just come to my attention. Please come in and shut the door."

Sheri tried to school her features as she entered the office but guessed she'd failed when he gave her another odd look. Was the tabloid conversation going to come up again?

She walked across the Italian marble floor to the thick Arabian carpet that lined the area in front of his desk. The Sabina Group was a first-class outfit all the way. No cheaply made faux-wood desks or cubicles for their offices. And Tristan's office was a lush as they came. She took a seat on one of the leather wingback chairs that he had for guests.

"Before you say anything, let me apologize for looking at that magazine earlier. Sorry about that. I couldn't resist seeing what Lucille was talking about."

He shook his head. "No need to apologize. I think I let my temper slip a bit when I saw what you were reading."

"Why?"

"The paparazzi are always following me around. They can be a real nuisance," he said.

He sounded almost bored, an air she knew he

used to hide his anger. "You've been making the headlines a lot, lately," she said.

"Our family always has. My grandmother was a famous actress in France, and my grandfather was a director. My family always generates a lot of interest."

"I'm sorry. I wish there was something I could do."

"Well, actually, there is."

"What?" She hoped he wasn't going to ask her to be some kind of paparazzi lookout. "I'm not sure the celebrity photographers who follow you are going to disappear if I ask them to."

"No?" He arched one eyebrow at her in a totally arrogant way, giving her a half smile that melted her brain.

"Maybe you should stop partying," she said before she thought better of it.

His lips twitched and he shrugged one of his shoulders in a very Gallic way. "Unfortunately it is too late for that." He rubbed the back of his neck. "I have a proposition for you, Ms. Donnelly."

"And that is?"

"A personal one."

"How personal?"

"Pretty personal."

"I thought it was important to you to keep things strictly business among everyone at the office," she said.

"Well, this is personal business. What would you say to an all-expenses-paid trip to the island of Mykonos in Greece?"

Her breath caught. "Tell me more," she said.

"One of my best friends is getting married there next week."

She stared at him, confused. "Do you want me to go in your stead?"

"No. I'm asking you to come with me and be part of the bridal party."

Come. With. Him. Oh, God, she wanted to jump up, say yes and leave before he changed his mind. Maybe he had noticed the real Sheri beneath the plain clothing. But she wasn't that naive. There had to be more to this than any kind of latent attraction.

"Why me?"

"The bride, Ava Monroe, is American."

"You know other Americans," she said, thinking of the actress.

"It's short notice and I want to bring someone I am comfortable with. Someone who won't be nosing around in Christos's business."

This wasn't the most flattering invitation she'd ever had. It reinforced something she knew but hated to face. That she wasn't a forever kind of girl. That men moved on, always leaving her behind. Starting with her father, the pattern had repeated again and again over the course of her life. She tried not to dwell on it or mope around, but sometimes she forgot and hoped…hoped that those little-girl dreams of a white knight would become reality.

She still wanted to say yes.

"Christos Theakis?"

"Yes. Do you know him?"

"Only what I've read about Christos and the Theakis heir in the papers." The Greek shipping tycoon had recently come to America and been photographed with a lovely woman and a young boy. The tabloids had speculated that the child was his secret son.

"What did the scandal rags say?"

"Not too much," she said, taken aback by the vehemence in his tone. She should change the subject. "What exactly does this proposition entail?"

He pushed to his feet and walked around his desk. He leaned back against the polished walnut surface, crossing his legs at the ankle.

"I want you to be my date for the week during

the wedding activities. They need a few women to round out the bridal party. The bride has one close friend she has asked, and she and Christos would like the groomsmen to invite the other attendants."

She stared at him for a minute, unsure she'd heard him right. She shook her head and opened her mouth, but no words came out. Then she closed her eyes. "Okay, did you say *date?*"

"That is correct."

Her eyes popped open. "Are you crazy?"

"Maybe. But I am serious about this."

"Serious about taking me to Greece for a week." She crossed her arms over her chest and settled back into the chair.

"Actually, ten days. And I already told Christos that you will be there."

"Shouldn't you have asked me before you started announcing that?" she asked, not even trying to keep the surprise from her voice.

He lifted one eyebrow at her. "I apologize. There wasn't time to discuss it with you. Christos just called to ask me and wanted a name to include in the wedding program. As my assistant, you were the first suitable woman to come to mind."

"Mr. Sabina—"

"Call me Tristan."

She stared at him. "Are you asking me because one of your lovers might get to thinking that marriage to you might be in the cards?"

He shrugged.

"Don't you care for any of them?"

"I care for all of them, but that isn't the point. I've had my once-in-a-lifetime love. Marriage is something I won't share with anyone else."

She'd heard through Lucille that he'd deeply loved his first wife, and that she'd died, but knew few other details. "Why not?"

"That's irrelevant. The only fact that concerns you is that I'd like you to accompany me to Greece for this wedding. It is a proposition, Sheri," he said in that low-toned voice of his. It was the first time he'd said her first name. He always addressed her as Ms. Donnelly.

"Like a business deal?" she asked.

"Yes, exactly. You do this for me and then I do something for you in return."

"What kind of favor?" she asked.

"Any. Your choice."

He seemed to have given this some thought. "I don't know. I'm not really that good at social stuff."

"I'll show you. That will be part of my favor to you."

"I'm still not sure... I can't make a decision like this so quickly."

"There is not much time. I'm leaving at 8:00 a.m. tomorrow on my jet.

"Sheri, I need you," he said, walking over to her and putting his hands on the arms of the chair. He leaned in close, and she shut her eyes as she breathed in the delicious scent of his aftershave.

He needed her. Oh, man, there was no way she was going to say no. Ten days of just her and Tristan... She couldn't resist the opportunity to get him to see her as more than just his assistant.

Two

The marriage of his best friend was a good reason to celebrate but, since Cecile's death, weddings had become painful for Tristan. Still…on this day, with the sun shining brightly in the Greek sky and the champagne flowing freely, he wasn't focused on the past.

In fact, as the reception progressed, he was becoming more and more obsessed with *Sheri*. He'd invited his assistant because he knew that bringing a real date to a wedding always made the woman start looking at him like he had the potential to be a husband.

He wasn't going down the aisle again.

Yet…there was something about Sheri that he found comforting. She was fun to work with, she was pleasing to look at it. Not a world-class beauty, but so unassuming about her looks that it was refreshing to be around her.

But today she looked exquisite. The pale bridesmaid's dress made her skin glow and the subtle makeup that someone had applied to her face gave her an understated beauty that he couldn't keep his eyes from. Seeing her move lithely through the stately, beautiful Theakis home and grounds where the wedding was being held had put her into a new light.

"You're staring at your secretary," Gui said as he came up behind Tristan.

"Am I?"

Gui arched one eyebrow at Tristan but said nothing more. Count Guillermo de Cuaron y Bautista de la Cruz was one of his two best friends, Christos Theakis, the groom, being the other member of their triad. They'd met at boarding school in Switzerland when they'd all been ten, three young hell-raisers who had nothing in common except being second sons, boys who'd grown up with no pressure or expectations.

In their twenties, they'd started a business called Seconds, a string of nightclubs in posh hot spots all over the world. The exclusive clubs were *the* place to see and be seen the world over, and every night the bouncers turned away more celebrities, wannabes and hangers on than they let in.

He heard the husky sound of Sheri's laughter and Lucille's familiar snort and smiled to himself. Lucille, who knew Christos well from working with Tristan for so long, had also flown up for the wedding, and the two women had hit it off in person. He wasn't really surprised, because Sheri was one of those women that everyone got along with, and she and Lucille had already been friendly via the phone.

He didn't examine too closely why he'd asked Sheri, and not Lucille, to be his companion for the wedding.

"You're staring again…are you falling for her?"

"Falling for who?"

"Your secretary."

"You know how I am. She's pretty and available."

"And that's enough for tonight," Gui said.

Tristan shrugged. He didn't like to talk about his attitude toward women. He had two sisters and had been married to the love of his life. If he'd been a different man with a different sex drive, he would have lived the rest of his life as a celibate. A part of him had died with Cecile.

But he had never been able to turn off his attraction to the opposite sex. Six months after her death, he'd found himself starting a string of one-week affairs. Sex was the only thing he'd ever take from the women he became involved with.

He suspected that would not be enough for Sheri. She also worked for him, and that complicated things. He shook his head and signaled the waiter for another glass of wine. The vintage was a very nice one from his family's vineyards.

"Tris?"

"Hmm?"

"She's not like your other women—"

"I know that, Gui."

Gui nodded. "I can't believe that Christos is married."

"It's not the death sentence you think it is." Though he'd never admit it, Tristan envied Gui his attitude. Gui had never been serious about one woman, and he moved through life with a kind of light charm that Tristan admired.

The music changed and a sweet, slow song came on. Couples filled the dance floor with Ava and Christos in the center. They seemed so… He shook his head, not willing to go there.

"I have to go," Gui suddenly said.

"Why?"

"Those men are too old for Augustina," Gui said, acting the protective older brother to his sister, who had been Gui's companion in the wedding party. Tristan bit back a smile as he watched his friend wedge his way between Augustina and her suitors.

He felt a small hand on his arm and glanced down at Sheri. "Having fun?" he asked.

"Yes. I can't believe I was reluctant to come," she said. Her breath smelled faintly of champagne. She held a half-empty glass in her right hand. She tucked her left hand between his arm and body.

She closed her eyes and swayed to the music. Just a little movement and humming under her breath.

"Are you enjoying the reception?" he asked.

"Yes, I am. Ava's so sweet. Thank you for inviting me to join you this week."

"You're welcome. I believe I owe you something."

"What do you owe me, Tristan?"

There was a dreamy quality to her voice. From the first it had been obvious to him that she was attracted to him. But she was careful to keep that attraction to herself and had put a barrier between them. Put him into a box, so it seemed. But tonight…tonight, with the trio playing romantic music and the wine flowing freely, none of that mattered.

"Dance with me, *ma douce?*"

She smiled up at him. "I'd love to."

He had never seen that exact look in her eyes before. "You seem different."

"Maybe that's because we're not in the office."

"No, we are not. What difference does that make to you, Sheri?"

"It makes all the difference in the world, Tristan."

She wrapped her arms around his shoulders and leaned up on tiptoe, brushing her lips against his neck. "This is so nice."

Tristan knew he should pull away and let her go but instead he leaned down, put his hand under her chin and tipped her head up toward his. His lips found hers easily and she sighed into his mouth as their lips met.

The wedding that she'd been nervous about participating in had taken on a certain dreamlike state. The champagne was good. Very good. There really was a difference between that stuff she bought in the grocery store and fine French champagne.

The music was chic and sexy and, as Sheri

leaned closer to Tristan, she realized that he was, too. His cologne was one of a kind and smelled delicious. She'd never get enough of it. Even at work the scent lingered in his office when he was away.

She knew it was partly the alcohol she'd drunk that gave the evening the magical quality that it was taking on as she danced with Tristan, but just this once she felt as if she was woman enough for him.

The right kind of woman for Tristan Sabina, international playboy, her boss and the sexiest man she'd ever danced with.

"What are you thinking?" he asked, his French accent nearly as appealing as the strong line of his jaw.

"About you."

"Really?"

"Um…yes. What are you thinking?"

"That maybe I should pull you closer," he said, suiting action to words.

She rubbed her cheek against his shoulder and closed her eyes. She knew this was another part of the wonderful dreamland she'd been in for the last week. Being on Mykonos was like being in a fantasy world.

Tristan and his friends were wealthy in every sense of the word and, when she was with them, she was living a life that was far removed from everything she'd ever known.

"Okay?"

"Yes," she said, her words a sigh. "Though I thought we'd decided that…um, we'd just have a professional relationship."

"Did we? I think we can both be forgiven for making the most of this moment, on a night like tonight."

She looked up at him, trying to judge if he was sincere, and she saw something in his eyes. Something she'd never seen in them before.

Lust.

Everything feminine in her clenched at that expression. Here was what she'd dreamed of. And how sad was it that she wanted to accept whatever he had to offer?

"For just this night?" she asked, to make sure she understood what he was offering.

"That's all I have in me," he said, but in his eyes she saw the hint of something more.

Some kind of emotion that intimated that he did feel more, but why did she care? Being in Tristan's arms was enough for her. This moment dancing together was better than she'd ever imagined it could be. She kept breathing deeply, trying to imprint the scent of him in her soul. She ran her hands down his shoulders and back, feeling the strength of his body under her touch.

If she were braver she'd press her body closer to his so she'd have the imprint of him against her to recall when she was back in the office and they were simply employer and employee again.

His finger under her chin startled her into opening her eyes and when he tipped her head back and their eyes met, she realized that there was more happening here than just a dance. She saw something else in Tristan's gaze. There was such sadness there, she thought. A kind of pain that she recognized all the way to her lonely soul.

Tristan Sabina, lonely?

The thought was ludicrous.

She shook her head. What the hell was she doing? This was her boss. She pulled back, put a respectable few inches between them, and he let her.

She got the message loud and clear. There *wasn't* more to this than Tristan feeling lonely at the reception and wanting…what exactly?

She tipped her head to the side as he brushed his finger along the line of her jaw. "Why are you looking at me like that?"

"I never realized how beautiful your eyes are."

She caught her breath. She wasn't beautiful and

she knew it. Her eyes were brown. Not the kind of luscious chocolaty color that poets wrote about, just plain brown. She shook her head.

"Yes, gorgeous. I could get lost in them."

"Tristan—"

He rubbed his thumb over her lower lip and her thoughts dissolved. She felt a tingling from that contact that spread down her neck and shoulders. And she realized that the safe little way in which she'd been obsessed with Tristan had turned into a dangerous and exciting attraction.

She knew that he wasn't himself tonight. That Monday morning, when they were back at work, they would return to the relationship they'd always had.

A sane person would turn around, walk off the dance floor and go back to her room.

But she'd been alone in her room for much of her life. In a box of her own making where she was safely insulated from pain. From the men who always left her.

She looked up at Tristan. He stared at her lips. His own parted as he stroked hers. And she wondered if knowing he was leaving, figuratively speaking, after one night would somehow lessen the pain of being left once again.

And she didn't kid herself that it wasn't going to be painful when he left. It was always painful, but being with Tristan…being in his arms and experiencing the things she'd dreamed of since the first time he'd walked into her office…well, that might be worth it.

Wouldn't it?

She didn't know and didn't want to analyze it. For once she wanted to forget that she was a plain-Jane kind of woman. That she was the kind of girl who usually went back to her room alone. For tonight, she was the woman that Tristan Sabina was looking at with lust in his eyes.

He and Sheri danced together for the rest of the evening and once Christos and his bride left, Tristan thought of leaving, too. But he glanced over at Sheri and was unable to walk away.

He drew her back out onto the dance floor, moving their bodies together. Feeling the rightness of the way she fit in his arms and against his body.

If she pulled back, of course he'd let her walk away. He had never had to coax a woman into his bed. But with Sheri, he was tempted. He was tempted to ply her with champagne and kisses.

Kisses.

He'd tasted her lips once, and now that was all he wanted to do. Stroke his tongue over the seam between her lips until she sighed and opened her mouth. Let his tongue sweep into the softness of her mouth. She would taste sweet…of champagne and something else that was uniquely Sheri.

He could not resist. He lowered his head, and she rose to meet him. She moaned into his mouth, wrapping her arms around his neck and leaning up on her tiptoes to keep their mouths together. He held her waist, lifting her against him. He felt the impact of her breasts against his chest and wanted to groan out loud. How could he ever have missed the fact that Sheri was a damned attractive woman?

He pulled back and looked down into those deep chocolate eyes of hers. They were wide and dreamy-looking. She brought one hand from his shoulder to her mouth and traced her lips with her forefinger.

"Sheri?"

"Hmm?"

"Would you like me to kiss you again?" he asked.

"Oh, yes," she said, licking her lower lip and leaning her weight on him as she stretched up toward him.

He bent lower and as soon as his lips brushed hers she opened her mouth and her tongue met his.

Just a soft, tentative touch, and then she made that little moaning sound and he felt the gentle edge of her teeth against his lower lip as she sucked him into her mouth.

He opened his eyes and saw that hers were closed and she was absorbed totally in the moment. He realized things were going too far for a public dance floor. Sheri's burgeoning passion was for him, and him alone.

Damn, he'd never felt this possessive about a woman before.

He lifted his mouth from hers, tucked her head into the curve of his neck and shoulder. Rubbed his hands down her back until he thought he could walk without each step being painful.

The crowd at the reception had thinned. The photographer from the Sabina Group was still there, but otherwise the event was paparazzi free. The guards that Christos had hired had provided an environment where his bride and his guests could relax and not have to worry about being pursued.

"Sheri?"

"Yes, Tristan?"

He couldn't ask her to stay with him tonight, he thought. This was his assistant. The woman he counted on to be cheeky and funny and to keep his

New York office running efficiently. Yet he wanted her, and he wasn't in the habit of denying himself anything he wanted.

"Did you like that?"

"Kissing you?"

"Mmm, hmm."

"Oh, yes. Very much. And dancing with you," she said, her eyes sparkling as she shimmied against him in time to the slow jazz number playing. "Did you enjoy it?"

"Kissing you or dancing with you?" he asked, just to tease her.

"Both."

"Yes."

She arched both eyebrows at him. "Really? I know you're used to more sophisticated women."

"How do you know that?" he asked. He never discussed his private life at the office.

"I searched you on Google. I read the *Post*. And Lucille sends me the French tabloids with pictures of you."

"Why?" he asked, realizing that Sheri was a lot more talkative when she drank. Normally, she'd try to play off her interest in him, but not tonight.

"You're my obsession," she said, her tone airy and breathless.

"Obsession?" he asked.

She flushed and pushed out of his arms. Her hands came up to cover her face. "Oh, my God. I can't believe I said that."

Tristan cupped her elbow and led her from the dance floor. Sheri grabbed a glass of champagne from a passing waiter. Taking a delicate sip, she drew to a stop.

"Will you please forget I said that?"

Not in a million years, he thought. She was totally unique in a world of women who fawned over him. There was a freshness to her. An innocence that he'd never experienced. Not even with Cecile, who'd been ten years his senior.

"Tristan? Did you hear me?"

"Yes, I did."

"And?"

"No, Sheri, I will not forget you said that."

"Why not?"

"Because I like being your obsession. What have you obsessed about doing with me?"

She shook her head and he wondered if she'd back down now. Instead she took a sip of her champagne and smiled up at him. "I'm not sure you're ready to know about that."

"When do you think I will be?"

She shrugged. Her delicate shoulders moved underneath the pretty silk straps of the bridesmaid's dress. "I'm not sure you'll ever be ready."

"Why not?"

"Because of what I said earlier."

"And that was?"

"You're not used to a woman like me."

"*Ma petite,* that I may not be, but I'm definitely ready for a woman like you."

Three

Sheri kept her hand in Tristan's as they walked toward the front of the mansion, where the valet was stationed, to get his car. Suddenly she hesitated, realizing that this was going to change her life. She forced herself to look around and acknowledge that, if she kept walking, her life *would* change.

"Sheri?"

She bit her lower lip, wondering if she was going to pass up the chance of a lifetime. And the answer was…she had no idea. She was torn between what she wanted—the man she'd wanted for so long—and self-preservation.

"Yes?"

"Would you like to stay here?"

No, she thought. But now she couldn't say that she was swept away by the moment. He was putting the onus on her, which was exactly where it should be. Clearly, he was leaving…and the thought of watching another man walk away was too much for her. The decision was made that easily.

She had no idea what the future would hold, but on this night she was going to be with Tristan. And it could only be this night, because she was flying back to the States in the morning.

"Where are you taking me?" she asked.

"My villa."

"You have a villa on Mykonos?"

"Yes. I own property all over the world," he said.

"Why? There's no real reason for you to be here for the magazine."

"One of my best friends lives here. Plus, in the summer, it's a nice place to holiday."

She nodded. "I don't own any property." She was very lucky that her brownstone in Brooklyn was a fixed-price rental. She'd taken over the lease upon her aunt's death.

He arched one eyebrow at her. "Is that important?"

She shrugged and realized that, to him, it wouldn't be. And unless she wanted to ruin the wonderful attraction that was flowing between the two of them, she needed to stop being so mired in who she was.

"It's not. So where is this villa?"

"Not far. Ready to go?"

She nodded.

She started forward but he stopped her with a hand on her arm, drawing her back against his chest. He leaned down and whispered something in French that she couldn't understand and kissed her neck.

Tingles of arousal spread down her body, tightening her nipples and making her breasts feel fuller. He wrapped his arms around her from behind, one hand at her waist, one hand right under her breasts.

She tipped her head to the side to give him better access to her throat. He whispered her name and kept her close to him before biting her softly and lifting his head.

He took her hand in his and led the way out of the building. They waited for the car. Tristan kept his gaze on the night sky. But Sheri couldn't help looking at him and marveling that, for tonight, he was hers.

Tristan Sabina is going to be mine. The future didn't matter at this moment, because she wanted him with the kind of keen longing she'd never experienced before with a man.

He turned to her and lifted one eyebrow as if he were asking her what she was thinking. She flushed and shook her head.

He smiled then lowered his head and kissed her, his lips feathering over hers and his hands skimming down the sides of her body. His fingers brushed against the curves of her breasts and came to rest at her waist, pressing her up into his body.

She liked the way he felt against her. His height made her feel delicate and very womanly. His hands were large enough to span her waist and she felt them wrap around her. Everything else dropped away.

There was just her and Tristan. His lips on hers, his hands on her body and the very essence of him seeping into her cold and lonely soul.

She suckled his lower lip, drawing it into her mouth. His hands tightened on her and his erection brushed against her lower belly. She swallowed hard and pulled back, looking up at him.

She had a little sexual experience, but nothing that had made her feel like Tristan was.

"What is it?" he asked, bringing one hand up to cup her cheek. His thumb stroked her skin and she looked up into his warm gray eyes and felt something shift inside her.

"Why me?"

"Why not you?"

She shook her head and realized that, if she asked questions, she should be prepared to hear an answer that might not be what she was searching for.

But she'd never been a coward, and this night with Tristan…well, she wanted to make the most of it. Be someone she'd never been before.

"Seriously, why are you making a move now?"

"That sounds so crass, *ma petite*. I have no ulterior motive. I have a beautiful woman in my arms and I don't want to let her go."

"I'm not beautiful," she said, because she knew it was true. There were truly beautiful people in the world and she wasn't one of them. She was more apt to be described based on her sterling personality. It wasn't that she was unattractive, it was just that there was nothing that really made her stand out.

"Tonight you sparkle," he said.

She felt her cheeks heat up with a blush. He lowered his head once again, kissing her, and in his arms she realized she did feel beautiful. She felt worthy to be on his arm as they got in his black Lamborghini and drove through the narrow streets of Mykonos.

He kept her hand on his thigh and his hand on top of hers, moving only to shift gears, and occasionally to lift her hand to his mouth to kiss the back of it.

She leaned her head back against the leather seat and turned to watch him. Tristan Sabina…she couldn't believe she was alone with him at last.

Tristan parked the Lamborghini behind his villa and got out. Sheri had her door opened before he got there. He offered his hand to help her out of the car. He saw the surprise in her eyes as she took it.

He realized that no one had ever been good to her in the way that men should be toward women. He wanted to change that, at least for tonight.

When she was standing next to him, he tucked a loose curl behind her ear. He couldn't get enough of touching her. He led the way into his house, tossing his keys on the kitchen countertop and hitting the light switch. She stood awkwardly just inside the doorway. Was this the moment when she'd change her mind?

He wouldn't pressure her into staying, he thought.

Then she nibbled on her lower lip and his entire body went on point. God, he wanted her. Why now?

He'd had a few inconvenient fantasies since they'd arrived here on Mykonos. Away from the office, Sheri had dropped her barriers and started to relax. He'd always liked her cheeky attitude, but seeing her in shorts on Christos's yacht during the week and tonight in this dress that actually fit her…well, it got to him.

He tried to remind himself that she was his assistant and that this was the kind of situation that Rene always warned him against. Fraternization was firmly frowned upon at the Sabina Group, especially by the CEO, Tristan's older brother, Rene.

And frankly, now that she was here in the villa, she seemed nervous. Not at all like the sexy woman he'd held in his arms on the dance floor.

"Would you like a drink?"

"No thank you," she said. "I… Show me your place."

He shrugged out of his tuxedo jacket and tossed it on the bar stool at the kitchen counter. He led her out of the kitchen into a formal reception room and up the stairs to the living room. He'd put on some music and dance with her again. That would relax her like nothing else would.

And he'd have her back in his arms.

"Look at the view," she said as they stepped into his living room. One wall was all windows, showcasing the view of the city of Mykonos and the Aegean Sea.

"It's even more spectacular from the balcony. Would you like to see that?"

She nodded.

He put his hand on the small of her back and lowered his mouth to hers and kissed her slowly. She shifted in his arms, turning to wrap her arms around his shoulders.

Blood rushed through his veins, pooling in his groin. He lifted his head. Her lips were wet and a little swollen from his kisses. "Come, let me show you the view."

He led her outside and the cool evening air surrounded them. She rubbed her hands over her arms. He brushed her hands aside, caressing her and pulling her back against his body.

He kissed her neck and shoulders as she stood still under his touches. Then she turned around and rose up on her tiptoes, taking his mouth with hers. Her tongue teased his and he realized that, though she was a little nervous, she was with him right now.

Wanting him the way he wanted her.

He felt her fingers at his neck, loosening his bow tie and then tossing it away. "Can I unbutton your shirt?"

"Yes."

She did with slow touches. "You have a great body, Tristan."

"How do you know?"

"I saw it in *People* magazine's spread on you last summer. A photo of you at the beach."

He growled deep in his throat when she leaned forward to brush kisses against his neck. Her lips were sweetly shy as she slowly unbuttoned his shirt. Then she nibbled her way lower, and he felt the edge of her teeth graze his skin.

He watched her, his eyes narrowing and his pants feeling damned uncomfortable. Her tongue darted out and brushed his nipple. He arched against her and put his hand on the back of her head, urging her to stay where she was.

She put her hands on his shoulders and eased her way down his chest. She traced the muscles that ribbed his abdomen and then slowly made her way lower. He could feel his heartbeat in his erection and he knew he was going to lose it if he didn't take control.

But another part of him wanted to let her have

her way with him. When she reached the edge of his pants, she stopped and glanced up his body to his face.

Her hand brushed over his straining length. "I guess you like that."

He muttered the French equivalent to the American "Hell, yeah," and pulled her to him. He lifted her slightly so that her breasts brushed his chest. "Now it is my turn," he said.

Blood roared in his ears. He was so hard, so full that he needed to be inside of her body *right now.*

Impatient with the fabric of her dress, he drew it up over her head and tossed it out of his way. No bra. He caressed her creamy thighs. God, she was soft. She moaned as he neared her center and then sighed when he brushed his fingertips across the *V* of her panties.

The cotton was warm and wet. He slipped one finger under the material and hesitated for a second, looking down into her eyes.

They were heavy-lidded. She bit down on her lower lip and he felt the minute movements of her hips as she tried to move his touch where she needed it.

He was beyond teasing her or prolonging anything. He pressed her panties aside, slipping two fingers into her humid body. She squirmed against him.

He pulled her head to his so he could taste her mouth. Her lips parted and he told himself to take it slow, that Sheri wasn't used to him. But one touch and he was out of control.

He held her at his mercy. Her nails dug into his shoulders and she pressed upward. He pulled away from her mouth, glancing down to see her nipples pushing against his chest. She closed her eyes and held her breath as he ran his finger over one nipple. It was velvety compared to the satin smoothness of her breast. He brushed his finger back and forth until she shifted on his lap.

He caressed her back, scraping a nail down the length of her spine to the indentation above her buttocks.

He wanted to give her so much pleasure, because he suspected she hadn't experienced true passion before.

Women were vulnerable when it came to sex. Not just in a physical way, but in an emotional one, as well, and Tristan made it a point to make sure that his lovers knew how sexy and beautiful he found them.

She moaned, a sweet sound that he captured in

her mouth. She tilted her head to the side immediately to allow him better access. She held his
shoulders and moved on him, rubbing her center
over his erection.

Gently he scraped his fingernail over her nipple
again and she shivered in his arms. He pushed her
back a little bit so he could see her. Her breasts
were bare, nipples distended and begging for his
mouth. He lowered his head and suckled.

He held her still with a hand on the small of her
back. He buried his other hand in her hair and
arched her over his arm. Both of her breasts were
thrust up at him. He had been with many women,
but he knew that he wanted Sheri more than he'd
wanted any other woman in a long time. What the
hell? This was sex, not about wanting her.

He wouldn't let this be about anything other
than the physical. One night together.

"Tristan?"

"Hmm?"

"Okay?"

Damn. He didn't want her out of the moment.
"I'm fine. Just enjoying you, *ma petite*."

Her eyes were closed, her hips moving subtly
against him, and when he blew on her nipple he
saw gooseflesh spread down her body.

He loved the way she reacted to his mouth on her breasts. Her nipples were so sensitive, he was pretty sure he could bring her to orgasm just from touching her there.

The globes of her breasts were full and fleshy, more than a handful. He licked the lily-white valley between them, suckling at her to leave his mark. He wanted her to remember this moment, what they had done, when she was alone later.

Soon her hands clenched in his hair and she rocked her hips harder against his length. He lifted his hips, thrusting up against her. He bit down carefully on one tender, aroused nipple. She cried his name and he hurriedly covered her mouth with his, wanting to feel every bit of her passion. He was so hard he thought he'd die if he didn't get inside her.

He glanced down at her and saw that she was watching him. The fire in her eyes made his entire body tighten with anticipation.

Since he'd always prided himself on being a conscientious lover, he knew he should ask about birth control, but that could be a mood killer with some women. So instead he reached for the condom he'd put in his pocket earlier before leaving for the reception. He'd planned to get laid so he could assuage the memories of his own wedding but he'd never anticipated he'd be here now with Sheri.

"Tristan." She said his name with the hint of shyness he'd noticed in her earlier.

"Yes," he said.

"I'm not…really good at this."

"You will be in my arms."

She shook her head. "Don't wait for me to… well, you know. It's hard for me."

"It won't be with me."

"Tristan—"

"Shh," he said, pulling her back into his arms and setting about arousing her again to the point where she would forget that she supposedly couldn't orgasm. Because of her cheeky attitude, he hadn't realized how innocent Sheri was. She seemed like a confident woman, comfortable with who she was, and only here on the balcony with her in his arms did he realize that she was as big a fraud as he was.

"Come to me now."

She reached between his legs and fondled him, cupping him in her hands, and he shuddered. He needed to be inside her now. He eased her panties off then shifted and lifted her thighs, wrapping her legs around his waist as he leaned back against the wall of the balcony. The sky was full of stars and the lights of Mykonos spread out below them. Her hands fluttered between them and their eyes met.

He held her hips steady and entered her slowly, deeply, pulling her down on him until he was fully seated. Her eyes widened with each inch he gave her. She clutched at his hips as he started thrusting. He leaned down and caught one of her nipples in his teeth, scraping very gently. She started to tighten around him. Her hips moved faster, demanding more, but he kept the pace slow, steady, wanting her to come before he did.

He suckled her nipple and rotated his hips to catch her pleasure point with each thrust, and he felt her hands in his hair clenching as she threw her head back and her climax ripped through her.

He varied his thrusts, finding a rhythm that would draw out the tension at the base of his spine. Something that would make his time in her body, wrapped in her silky limbs, last forever.

He turned them around so that she was pressed against the wall, then he tilted her hips, giving himself deeper access to her body. She scraped her nails down his back, clutched his buttocks and drew him in. He tightened, and his blood roared in his ears as he felt everything in his world center on this one woman.

He called her name as he came. She tightened around him and he looked down into her eyes as he kept thrusting. He saw her eyes widen and felt the minute contractions of her body around his as she was consumed by another orgasm.

He rocked his hips against her until she stopped moving. She wrapped her arms around his shoulders and kissed the underside of his chin.

"Thank you."

"For what, *ma petite?*"

"For giving me this night. It's like something out of one of my dreams."

With those words she brought him completely out of himself and into a place he'd been only once before. A place of vulnerability that he'd hoped never to find again.

Four

Tristan carried her back into the villa. Sheri didn't get a chance to look at the place though, as he carried her straight to the bedroom.

He put her on her feet next to the bed.

As she stood naked in front of him, he traced the strawberry birthmark on her right hip. She felt so vulnerable, standing with him looking at her. He'd refastened his pants and his shirt hung open, but he was still essentially dressed and she was naked.

She crossed her arms over herself, one across her breasts, the other over her lower body.

"What are you doing?" he asked, his voice deeper than normal, his French accent more pronounced.

"I'm not…"

"Not what?"

"I look better with clothes on," she said at last.

He shook his head. "Not those baggy frocks you wear in the office."

"You don't like the way I look at work?"

He traced his finger over the edge where her right arm covered her breasts. His finger dipped beneath her arm to caress the upper curves of her breast. "I like the way you look. It is those frumpy clothes you wear that I don't like."

"Frumpy?"

"Yes."

"I'm not good with fashion," she said, not sure why she was telling him this. In the darkened bedroom, with her body still tingling from the incredible orgasms he'd helped her achieve, she felt oddly relaxed. If only she was wearing something. "Why don't you take your shirt off?"

"Would you like me to?"

"Yes, definitely."

He shrugged out of it, and she reached for it before he could toss it aside. She put her arms in the sleeves, but he held the two sides open. "I like you naked."

"I feel too exposed."

"Why?"

She felt more vulnerable now than she had just a second before. She just shrugged.

He didn't say anything else, just bent to trace her birthmark with his tongue. Could he want her again so soon?

She couldn't think as he stood back up and lifted her onto the bed. He slipped off his pants and underwear, then bent down to capture the tip of her breast in his mouth. He sucked her deep, his teeth lightly scraping against her sensitive flesh. His other hand played at her other breast arousing her, making her arch against him in need. Yes, he could.

She reached between them and took his erection in her hand, bringing him closer to her, spreading her legs so that she was totally open to him. "I need you now."

He lifted his head. The tips of her breasts were damp from his mouth and very tight. He rubbed his chest over them as he slid deep into her body.

She moved her hands down his back, cupping his butt as he thrust deeper into her. Their eyes met. Staring deep into his eyes made her feel as if their souls were meeting. She felt her body start to tighten around him, catching her by surprise. She climaxed before him. He gripped her hips, holding her down and thrusting into her two more times before he came with a loud groan of her name.

He held her afterward, disposing of the condom but then pulling her into his arms and tucking her up against his side.

She wrapped her arm around him and listened to the solid beating of his heart. She fought to remember that this was just for one night. Men leave, she reminded herself firmly. But, lying in his arms, she felt as if this could last forever. She burrowed closer to him, holding him tightly to her.

She wished she could say that she understood him better now than she ever had before. But she had the feeling that she'd simply revealed her own weaknesses. Showed how little she felt she was worth.

"Are you sleeping?" he asked.

She felt the vibration of his words in his chest and under her ear. She shifted in his embrace, tipping her head so she could see the underside of his jaw.

"No. Too much to think about." This had been the most exciting day of her life. She felt as though, if she went to sleep, she might wake up and find none of it had happened. He traced his fingertips over her body, starting at her forehead and moving slowly down. She felt him linger on the birthmark, tracing over it again and again.

He tipped her head up so that their gazes met. "Thank you for coming to Mykonos this week."

"You're welcome. I enjoyed it."

"Was the vacation what you thought it would be?"

She pushed herself up on one elbow, looking down at his dark features and tracing her finger over his brows. "I can safely say it wasn't at all what I expected it to be."

"Better?"

"Yes." She paused. "Thank you for wearing a condom," she said. "I'm not on the pill."

"No problem."

It bothered her that he'd had condoms on him. That spoke volumes about the differences in their attitudes toward sex and sex partners.

"I don't think either of us wanted to deal with an unexpected pregnancy."

"You're right." His words were a stark reminder to her that this was a one-night stand. No matter that he hadn't said anything; she could read between the lines. Though his attitude toward pregnancy was one she shared. When she was eighteen, she'd vowed she'd never have children. She'd been too young to make that kind of decision, but the emotions behind it had been real.

Sheri still slept in his arms. Tristan glanced at his watch. They were flying back to the States later this afternoon. Because he wanted to linger, he pushed himself out of bed. He wanted to pull her into his arms and hold her tightly to him so that he knew she'd stay right by his side. And he'd only ever wanted to stay in bed with Cecile.

"Tristan?"

"Right here," he said. He sat on the side of the bed with his back to her, because if he saw her in his bed one more time he'd make love to her again. And he needed to start building a distance between them again. Last night was fine, but this morning he needed to get her dressed and out of his villa.

"Is it morning already?" she asked, leaning up to kiss his shoulder blade.

He shifted away from her on the bed, putting some distance between them.

"Yes."

In the silence that followed, he sensed her confusion.

Her stomach growled, breaking the tension, and he laughed. "Hungry?" He dared a glance at her.

She buried her red face under the sheet. "Yes. I was too nervous to eat last night."

"Why nervous?"

"Ava wanted her wedding to be perfect and I didn't want to screw it up. And Augustina is gorgeous, as is Ava's maid of honor, Laurette. I was the only weak link in the wedding party."

"You were gorgeous, too," he said glancing over his shoulder at her again.

She was this morning, too, with her thick hair hanging around her shoulders. She didn't have a speck of makeup on, but the beauty that he'd somehow never noticed because of her ugly clothes now shone through.

She shook her head. "I'm not, but thank you for saying that."

She wrapped the sheet around her torso and leaned up, embracing him from behind. She kissed the junction where his neck and shoulder met. "Thank you for last night."

To hell with restraint. He pulled her around on his lap. Felt her hips brush his morning erection. He kissed her forehead. "Thank *you,* Sheri."

She hugged him. Just put her arms around him and held him close. And he knew that no matter what happened he didn't want to hurt her. He wanted to believe that he could find a way to make sure she didn't regret being with him.

"Have you thought about doing anything else at the magazine?"

She pushed away from him, sitting on the bed next to him. "I can't work for you anymore?"

He got to his feet and found his pants, pulling them on quickly. "Of course you can continue to work for me. But I wondered if you'd ever considered an editorial job, or sales?"

"Tristan?"

"Hmm," he said without turning to face her.

"Look at me please."

He turned, hands on his hips. "Yes?"

"I don't expect anything from you after this. This was just two people who hooked up at a wedding reception."

He doubted she was aware of how transparent her face was, or how she'd flinched when she said *hooked up*. He scrubbed his hands over his face. The morning sunlight seeped in under the wooden blinds that covered the windows, painting the room in cheery colors. But instead of seeing the promise of a new day, all he felt were last night's regrets.

He knew better than to take Sheri to his bed. She

wasn't like the women he usually dated. "We were friends before this."

"We were acquaintances," she amended. "And we'll go back to being them again. Don't worry about me. I might not be as used to this situation as you, but I can handle it."

He had no doubt that Sheri could handle anything that came her way. She was strong like that. "Very well. Would you like to take a shower while I see about breakfast?"

"You can cook?" she said, with the cheeky grin he'd come to know so well.

He flushed at the way she said it. "No, but my housekeeper can."

"What's on the menu?"

"Whatever you like," he said. Mrs. Thonnopulus was very skilled in the kitchen and he had no doubt she'd be able to fix anything that Sheri asked for.

"Raisin Bran and some coffee would be great."

He nodded. "We'll have breakfast on the balcony. I'll use the guest bathroom down the hall."

She shook her head. "Don't be silly. I can use that one." Then she turned bright red and looked around his room. "I'm going to need something to wear."

"I'll bring in some clothes for you. You wear a size six in the States?"

"Yes, I do. But…whose clothes are they?"

"My sister's." Thanks to Blanche, he had grown up in a household where discussions had routinely centered on fashion. He knew equivalent sizes. "Go and shower. I'll leave the clothes on the bed."

She nodded and tugged the top sheet completely free from the bed, wrapping it around her. She looked small standing there, and vulnerable.

He turned away before he did something else he'd regret, or said something he knew he couldn't possibly mean, because he never dated a woman for more than a week. He usually only took them to his bed for a night or two and then moved on.

Sheri was no different.

He wondered exactly how many times he was going to have to say that before he started believing it.

Sheri stood on the threshold between the living room and the balcony. Looking out, she saw the place where she'd made love with Tristan for the very first time. Her body was sensitive this morning, remembering the feel of him against her—inside her.

She shook her head, trying to force the images

of Tristan making love to her from her head. She wished she could forget him easily. Get the distance she knew she'd need before they were both back in the office on Monday morning.

Yet, at the same time, she didn't want the feeling of having his body inside hers to fade.

Tristan stood by the railing. He was on his cell phone, and he gestured for her to sit at the wrought iron table that was set for breakfast for both of them. He wore a pair of black dress pants and a short-sleeved, casual shirt. He looked suave, debonair, and she felt… Well, even in the sophisticated clothing he'd provided for her, she still felt a bit frumpy.

There was a plate of croissants with jam and butter, the cereal she'd requested but in European packaging with a different name than she was used to in the States, and a small French press coffeepot.

She fiddled with her hair, tucking it behind her ear, waiting for him to look back at her. And when he did, she wished he hadn't. There was too much knowledge in his eyes. It was clear that he knew she wasn't herself this morning.

Tristan put his hand over the phone. "I have to finish this call and I'll join you in a moment."

"No problem. I can take care of myself."

He gave her that steely-eyed look of his, but she ignored him as she seated herself.

"I'll be right back. Wait for me to eat?"

"If you'd like me to," she said, but inside a panic was starting. She wanted to forget about breakfast and get away as fast as she could. She also wanted to linger. Wanted him to be sitting here waiting for her. Maybe kiss her when she'd come out instead of being on the phone.

But that was just more of the fantasy she'd always wanted, and this was reality. One-night stands weren't the beginning of a romance. They were temporary.

Temporary.

Maybe if she said the word enough times she'd start to realize that her reality wasn't with Tristan.

Too bad she remembered the way he'd held her last night even when they were sleeping. There was some kind of closeness between them that she didn't want to let go.

"I would."

She nodded as he walked away. Watch him, she told herself. Watch him walk away and know that he's not the kind of man who'll stay. Temporary, she reminded herself again.

But dammit, she wanted him to be. Last night she realized that she'd been trapped in a box of her own making, that she'd let the men in her life dictate how she moved through life.

Last night she'd stepped outside of that box.

Instead of feeling unworthy of a man's attention, she'd felt as if she deserved to be with Tristan. She wasn't kidding herself that he might be the man for her. Their lives were too different. But he had changed her, and as she poured a cup of black coffee she realized she didn't want to go back to being the woman she'd been before.

It was time she started living.

She took another sip of her coffee and felt that nervous anticipation that came from waiting. It reminded her so clearly of the times she'd sat in front of Aunt Millie's house, waiting for her dad to show up. And he never did.

God, she was pitiful. She pushed to her feet and walked away from the table, taking her coffee mug with her. She went to the railing and looked down at the street. It was crowded this morning with cars and people. Strange for a Sunday.

A man glanced up at the balcony and took a photo. She shook her head, knowing he was capturing the architecture of Mykonos and not her.

She stepped back from the railing so that he could get a better picture.

"Come inside," Tristan said, and something in his tone put her on edge.

"What? Why?"

"We have to talk."

Man, she hoped he wasn't going to fire her. If he did, she could find another job as an executive assistant somewhere else in the city, but starting over was always hard.

"Let's talk here," she said.

"No. Come inside now."

"Why are you—"

"Sheri, inside now."

"Tristan, you can't speak to me like that. I'm not your pet or slave."

"I don't think of you that way. Things have happened. Come inside and I will explain."

"Is it Christos and Ava? Are they okay?"

"Yes, they are fine," he said, reaching for her elbow and drawing her into the living room. He closed the door behind her and then clicked a button on the remote in his hand. The blinds slid slowly down, covering the windows.

"If this is how you always behave the morning

after, I finally understand why women only stay with you for a short while."

"Sheri, this is serious."

"I was being serious," she said, knowing that she had to find a way back to being his humorous assistant.

"You are being cheeky and another time I'd appreciate that, but not right now."

He was starting to scare her. "Tristan, I can… Listen, it won't be weird at work. I'm not going to be all clingy or anything."

"I know you won't be."

"You're going to fire me?"

He crossed his arms over his chest and gave her a narrow look.

"I can handle it, honestly. I just need to know what I'm facing."

"You're not facing anything," he said, tossing her a newspaper. A Greek tabloid. "We'll face this together."

She saw the photo of herself naked in Tristan's arms as they were kissing on the balcony.

Five

Sheri had never wanted to be famous. Unlike other kids who dreamed of celebrity, she'd preferred her natural anonymity, so as she stared down at the newspaper in front of her, skimming the headline written in a language she couldn't read, she saw only her picture.

Her face got hot as she blushed harder than she ever had before. She was going to die. That was it. There was no way she was going to live through this.

It was bad enough that she'd made the highly questionable decision to sleep with her boss. But now the entire world would know… Hell, *Lucille* would know, and she wasn't going to let Sheri forget about this.

"Oh, my God."

"I don't think praying will help," Tristan said in a quiet voice.

"What do you recommend?" she asked, desperately wishing she could go back in time.

He put a hand on her shoulder. It was big and warm and as he squeezed so slightly, she felt a little better. Not much, mind you, with her face and the ecstasy she'd felt in his arms clearly on display for the world to see.

Tristan's expression wasn't visible, as his face was buried in her hair. Her hands shook as she looked at the picture.

"I don't look like myself," she said, tracing a finger over her face. Her eyes were half-closed and she was clutching at Tristan as he kissed her. Thank goodness his broad shoulders covered her naked chest fairly well.

He reached around her to take the paper. "You look like a woman in the arms of her lover."

"Yeah, ya think?" Sheri said, unable to help herself. She wished she could get good and mad. But this wasn't Tristan's fault. It was only that fact that was helping her keep it together. That and the strong belief that if she let go of her control she was going to crumple to the floor and never get up.

"Cheeky is cute, Sheri. Sarcastic is not," he said, his accent very strong and pronounced.

She hated when he did that arrogant thing. Actually it was attractive at times, but right now, while she was grappling with the shock of seeing her scandalous picture in a major newspaper, it wasn't.

"Sleeping with you was fun while it was our little secret," she said, mirroring his tone. "Having the entire tabloid-reading world know about it is not."

"Sheri—"

She cut him off and turned away, walking farther into the elegantly appointed living room. She stood underneath a painting, a large oil by someone famous, she was sure, but she didn't know art. Her aunt Millie's taste had run more to prints of the Brooklyn Bridge than real art.

"Sorry, was that too sarcastic? I'm not used to dealing with the paparazzi the way you are."

"You're right," he said. "This is my mess. I will take care of this."

"How, exactly?" she asked.

"Leave it to me."

"Do they know my name?" She pivoted to

face him. The morning sunlight streamed
through the glass doors behind him, keeping his
face in shadow.

Tristan lifted the paper and read the article.

"You haven't read it yet?" she asked.

"Not all of it."

"What does the headline say?"

"'Snagged. Elusive bachelor found in love nest.'"

"Oh, my *God*."

"If you're going to pray, you should at least ask
for something."

"Tristan, I'm going to ask for lightning to
strike you."

"Not a wise course of action," he said.

"You don't think so?" she asked, trying to keep
the panic she felt rising inside her from her voice.

He wrapped his arm around her waist and drew
her into his body. "I don't. You need me, Sheri Donnelly, and I'm going to get you out of this mess."

This close to him, it was hard to keep the distance she'd been struggling to maintain since she
came down for breakfast.

"I can't believe this," she said.

"What?"

"I took a chance last night… Man, I knew that
leaving the reception with you was a bad idea, but

I was only thinking about what you might think when you saw me naked."

Tristan drew back and tipped her head up toward his. "What I might think when you were naked?"

"Yeah, you know, stuff like, 'she's a lot flabbier than the women I'm used to....'"

"*Ma petite,* you were perfection in my arms last night."

"You don't have to lay it on that thick, Tristan. I look in the mirror every day and what I see staring back at me isn't perfection."

"Your mirror is not the best. Otherwise you'd never leave your flat in the clothes you wear."

"Um…are you trying to make me feel better?" she asked.

He gave her a quick pat on the backside and stepped away. "I was, smart-ass."

"So how are we going to deal with this?"

"*We* are not. I am."

She shook her head. No way was she going to leave everything to Tristan. Thus far he hadn't exactly been successful in getting the paparazzi off his own tail. And she wasn't like him. She couldn't afford a security detail, or a chauffeur. She took the subway to work and walked seven blocks from the station to her office.

"Tristan—"

"Enough. I said I will deal with it. Trust me."

Tristan wasn't surprised by the flash of temper in Sheri's eyes. But he was surprised that she backed down. She crossed her arms over her chest, and he saw tears gleaming in her pretty brown eyes.

He was angry. At himself for not anticipating that photographers would be bold enough to take advantage of an intimate moment. At Sheri for looking up at him with wounded doe eyes that made him realize he *had* to fix this. She simply wasn't as sophisticated as the heiresses and actresses he usually brought to his bed, and laughing off this kind of scandal was beyond her.

And mostly he was mad at the tabloid that had decided to print this picture. He suspected it was because the publisher, Gabrielle Damienne, was an ex-lover of his and they hadn't parted on the best of terms.

"Sheri?"

"Yes."

"Will you trust me?" he asked.

Distantly he heard the doorbell ring, but knew the housekeeper would answer it. He had the feeling that anyone who came to the door today he wasn't going to want to see.

"I'm not sure."

Was her trust really important to him? She was more than a one-night stand, she was a woman he cared for, but he wasn't going to love her. So was trust really that important?

Yes, he thought. He wanted her to say she trusted him to handle this for her. He wanted to demand it. To make her admit that she would rely on him to handle this media mess.

"You seemed sure last night."

She narrowed her eyes and then tipped her head to the side. "Last night was lust. Surely you knew that."

He felt the burn of her words and that sickly sweet tone she used. He knew he'd been rushing her out the door until he'd seen the paper. He hadn't really cared if she'd picked up on that fact earlier. But now, hearing those words come from her lips...he realized he already cared more for Sheri than was prudent.

She was dangerous because she made him feel way more than lust for her sexy little body, which she kept hidden under the ugliest clothing he'd ever seen on a woman.

Today, dressed in his sister Blanche's blouse

and trousers, she looked…almost beautiful. Actually, the only thing detracting from her beauty were those wounded eyes of hers. She was hurting, and a different man, a man who still had a romantic heart, would soothe her.

There was a rap on the door. "Mr. Sabina?"

"Please come in."

Mrs. Thonnopulus opened the door. "I'm sorry to interrupt, sir, but Count de Cuaron y Buatista de la Cruz is here to see you."

Gui. He must have seen the paper this morning. And Tristan was glad to have his friend interrupt this situation with Sheri, which was going from bad to worse.

"Send him in."

Less than a minute later Gui strode through the door. Wearing jeans and a designer one-of-a-kind shirt, Gui looked relaxed and casual. Not like the aristocrat he was, but more like the second son he also was.

"Ms. Donnelly, Tristan, please pardon my unscheduled visit. But I need a word with you, Tris."

"About?"

"A sensitive matter," Gui said.

"Does it involve the photos of us in the newspaper?" Sheri asked, all blunt American.

Tristan wanted to order her from the room so he could have a discussion with Gui without her sarcasm.

"Indeed. So you've already seen the papers."

"Papers?"

"Reuters picked up the photo. It's in every tabloid I've been able to put my hands on this morning," Gui said.

Sheri started trembling. She turned her back on both men and dropped her head down to her chest. Tristan watched her, knowing she was dealing with the pain and unable to make himself walk across the room and comfort her.

He'd done enough of that this morning. He needed to keep a distance between them.

Gui arched one eyebrow at him and nodded toward Sheri. Tristan shrugged his shoulders and shook his head. Gui rolled his eyes and went to Sheri's side. He wrapped one arm around her shoulder and handed her a snowy-white handkerchief.

And Tristan saw red. It was that simple. He knew he'd just dismissed her, but he couldn't stand to see Gui touching Sheri. She was his. *His.*

He was across the room before he realized he was moving. He nudged Gui aside and pulled

Sheri into his arms. She put her head on his shoulder and he felt the warmth of her tears sinking through the cotton fabric of his shirt.

A wave of total helplessness swamped him. How was he going to fix this? He'd spent the last eight years since Cecile's death moving forward, never stopping to answer questions or challenge the paparazzi that followed him and the scandals he wove effortlessly.

He wrapped his arms around her and held her the way he hadn't held a woman in eight long years. He held her to give comfort. He felt the shackles he'd tried to wrap around his heart shift.

He lifted her face to his, aware that Gui had stepped out to the balcony to afford them some privacy at this moment.

"*Ma petite,* stop your tears."

"I… Yes, I will. It's just, I have no idea how to handle this," she said, sniffling delicately.

Damn those big doe eyes of hers, he thought. He wiped her cheek with his thumbs, brushed them down her face until the tracks from her tears were completely gone.

Step away, he told himself. Comfort was one thing, but kissing her now would be the kind of mistake he was too smart to make.

He'd started to lower his head, wanting to taste her one last time, and she rose on her tiptoes, eyes closing, and leaning into his body. And he knew that for her sake, so that he didn't hurt her any more than he already had, he couldn't kiss her.

So instead he brushed his lips against her forehead and stepped back. He turned away, but not quickly enough to miss the disappointment and hurt on her face.

Sheri had to get out. When Tristan turned his back and walked to the balcony, where she saw Gui waiting, she grabbed her handbag and made a beeline for the door. Enough of staying here. She was clearly not wanted.

And she had experienced more than enough of that in her life. She needed to move. She checked for her hotel-room key and her passport. Both were in her handbag. She also had enough money to pay for a cab.

She wondered if she should take the time to ask the housekeeper to call one for her or just take a chance at flagging one down on the street.

She heard the rumble of Tristan's and Gui's voices and knew that hanging around wasn't going to work for her. She was probably going to cry again, which was a stupid "girl" reaction to the situation, but she was tired. And she'd made love—no she'd *had sex*—with a man she'd been fantasizing about for too long. And now the entire world would know.

The only silver lining she saw was that Aunt Millie was dead and wouldn't see the picture.

She walked down the stairs to the ground floor and paused in the kitchen, looking around and re-membering how excited she'd been when she'd followed Tristan through this room.

How very much she'd wanted that man.

And he'd wanted her, she thought. At least for one night.

She opened the kitchen door and stepped out-side into a perfect February morning. Or at least, perfect on the island of Mykonos. It was a resort town. A place the trendy visited.

She should have felt out of place all week but there had been something very welcoming in Tristan's group of friends. Ava had made her feel so at ease, but then again the other woman was an American and had somehow recognized the at-traction that Sheri felt for Tristan.

"Mademoiselle?"

"Miss?"

"Hey, lady?"

The cries came at her from every corner as a group of photographers moved closer to her. She scrambled backward, reaching for the handle on the kitchen door. She tried to open it but her hands were sweating and she couldn't get a good grip.

She covered her face with her hands, took a deep breath and then opened her mouth and screamed the way she'd been taught to in self-defense class. A deep-throated loud sound that actually stopped the questions that the photographers were throwing at her in every language imaginable.

Asking her name. What kind of lover Tristan was. Did she think she'd finally snagged the elusive bachelor?

The door opened behind her and she felt Tristan's arm come around her waist as he drew her back into the kitchen and slammed the door closed.

She glanced up, thinking to thank him, but he looked so angry. So…not in the mood to be teased. She'd had no idea he could ever look that mad.

"What were you thinking? Why would you leave the house without my permission?" he asked.

She backed away from him but he put his hands on her shoulders and held her in place.

"I want answers, Sheri. This isn't a game. The paparazzi are going to be all over you until this blows over."

"I needed to get away," she said.

"From me?"

She nodded. "I…I like you way too much to be your plaything."

Tristan cursed under his breath, using the few French words she'd become very familiar with since he used them regularly in the office.

"*Merde* is right. I'm trying to be cool about this whole thing but…I'm not ready to this morning. I'm tired and my body still tingles from the last time we made love, and you were pushing me out the door this morning."

She tucked a strand of her curly hair behind her ear and looked up at him from under her eyelashes. His expression was unreadable.

"So I was trying to leave," she said, concluding as quickly as she could.

Tristan turned away from her, leaning back against the wall and crossing his arms over his chest. "First of all, I'm not expecting you to be blasé about sleeping with me."

"Well, that's good. Because I'm not."

He started to speak, but she held up her hand. She couldn't bear to hear him say that she was one of many to him. "I don't expect you to feel the same."

He shook his head.

"I can still feel you on my body, *ma petite.* The remembered feel of your sheath clasping me is making it damned hard for me to let you go."

"Oh."

"Yes, oh. Maybe you don't know quite everything."

She looked down. "I never meant to imply that I did."

He nodded. "Good. Then stop trying to manage this on your own. We need to deal with this together, or else you're going to get hurt."

She wrapped her arms around her waist before realizing what she was doing. The move was a dead giveaway that she felt vulnerable, and Tristan already had seen her with tears in her eyes. She knew him well enough to know that weakness wasn't something he understood.

He was immune to that flaw. And if he wanted her by his side, wanted them to be a team, she wanted to be worthy of staying with him.

This was the first time a man had come after her

and brought her back. The first time a man hadn't walked away from her, or simply let her walk away.

She knew better than to read too much into it, but she felt her heart beat a little faster.

Six

The getaway was simple. Gui, Sheri and Tristan left together via Tristan's dark-windowed Mercedes sedan, which the housekeeper drove to the private airport where the Seconds corporate jet waited for them. They had decided that Sheri would accompany Tristan to Paris and then back to Manhattan instead of getting on the commercial flight straight back to New York that he'd booked for her return.

She'd lost that wounded-doe look and smiled at him whenever he looked at her—which wasn't as often as he would have liked, but ignoring her was the only way he could even pretend to himself that he wasn't starting to care for her.

In that moment when they'd heard her scream, he'd felt fear for another person for the first time in eight years. And the fact that he'd wanted to first protect her and then rip apart the photographers who had threatened her, had been a warning Tristan couldn't ignore.

Despite the fact that he knew Gui was right and the only way to protect Sheri was to keep her by his side, another part of him—the man who'd experienced the crushing blow of losing the only woman he'd ever loved—wanted her far away from him.

"Have you been to Paris before?" Gui asked Sheri.

"No, never. This trip to Mykonos was the first time I've been out of the U.S."

"You should travel more," Gui said. "Tristan, you should make sure that Sheri has the opportunity to see the world. Do you know she still lives in the same brownstone that she was raised in?"

Since he wasn't deaf and the corporate jet wasn't a jumbo one, he'd heard the details of her life as Gui pried into her past. He knew it was Gui's way, but he hated the attention that his friend was giving to Sheri. And hated even more the way she soaked it up. She was hungry for a man to talk to her.

"I heard."

"It's in Brooklyn."

"Thanks, Gui. I know where my assistant lives," he said.

Sheri flushed and he saw her sink deeper into her chair. He'd crossed a line with that comment. He didn't need to put her back into the employee role at this moment.

Gui gave him a sharp look and turned back to Sheri, telling her about his latest escapade with one of his cousins who was at the Spanish royal court.

She laughed, but the sound was hollow and he knew he'd done that. Taken away her joy by being a complete ass. He should apologize but, when she was ignoring him, he knew that they were both moving apart. The way they needed to.

But dammit to hell, if Gui didn't move away from her, he was going to leap across the aisle and strangle his friend. "Sheri, when you have a moment I'd like to discuss a few things with you."

"What about?"

"Work. Our delay in returning to the office will mean rescheduling some appointments."

"Of course. I didn't bring my laptop with me…."

"You can log in on mine," he said.

"Surely that can wait," Gui said.

Sheri patted Gui on the arm. "No, it can't. I don't mind working. It'll give me something to occupy my mind."

Sheri moved across the aisle so that she was sitting in one of the captain's chairs and she turned it to face him. He turned his laptop around on the built-in desk. She leaned forward, a lock of her hair slipping free and brushing against her face.

She concentrated on typing her log-in to the network and then her password.

He leaned back in his leather chair and watched her work. Since this was the corporate jet owned by Seconds, there were three distinct areas. Gui's area, where Sheri had been sitting, was decorated in a classic style very much befitting an aristocrat. There was something quite traditional about Gui underneath his rebel exterior.

Christos's area was modern and sleek. Eschewing anything traditional due to a severe disagreement with his father when he was eighteen, Christos always chose things that wouldn't fit the traditional Greek way of life that his father, Ari, wanted for him.

Tristan's area was a blend of modern and classical. His desk had been handed down to him by his grandfather. It was old, though well polished, and except for two marks, looked to be in perfect condition. There was a small ink stain near the hole where an inkwell was once kept, and under the blotter was a series of initials. Each Sabina who inherited it added theirs to the line.

For all that he was a second son, he wasn't like Christos, who hated his family's traditions. He liked knowing his place in the Sabina line. But then, he had sisters and a large pool of cousins. Christos had recently lost his only brother in a plane crash.

"When do you anticipate being back in Manhattan? You have two video conferences scheduled this week. Rene could handle them in your place."

"I saw those e-mails, too. I think we need to get Maurice on the phone to talk through the book for *Global Traveler.* The new layout is supposed to start in the next issue, and I'm still not satisfied with the changes."

Sheri typed as he talked. He knew she was jotting down notes. He did like how efficient she was. Even before they'd been lovers, he'd liked watching her work. Her fingers were long and elegant. He would have said they were the most attractive part of her, before he'd seen her last night.

Her body was exquisitely formed with generous curves, but not overblown. And she'd been—

"Tristan?"

"Hmm?"

"I asked if a conference call will be fine? We can get the book scanned into a PDF and have it available this afternoon."

"Yes, that is fine," he said, and turned his attention to work. It was the one safe thing they had between them, and he knew that, when they landed at Le Bourget airport in Paris, he'd once more be focusing on the woman and not his executive assistant.

Tristan's sister Blanche waited for them in the chauffeur-driven Mercedes at the airport. Sheri immediately wanted to hide back on the plane. But that was cowardly and she'd... Well, she wasn't going to do it, no matter how tempted she might be.

"*Bonjour,* Tristan," Blanche said, embracing him. She continued speaking in French, which Sheri couldn't follow at all when the speaker was talking as quickly as Blanche was.

It was clear from her tone that she was upset with Tristan and reading him the riot act. Sheri stood in the shadows and watched the two interact. She saw the affection beneath the lecture.

And Tristan smiled down at his sister indulgently. Sheri watched the two of them longingly. She'd always wanted a big family. Not necessarily blood relatives, but a network of people who cared deeply for her and let her do the same for them. It was clear that Tristan had that.

Watching him with Gui and Christos over the last week had given her a glimpse into that world. Seeing him with his sister added another dimension.

"Why are you hiding over here?" Tristan asked, coming back to get her. "Blanche wants to meet you."

She took a deep breath. "I wasn't hiding. I wanted to give you a moment alone with your sister."

"I appreciate that."

"It looked like she was lecturing you. I didn't think you'd tolerate that from anyone," Sheri said, without really thinking.

Tristan smiled, and for the first time she realized that he usually had a practiced smile for business, because this one lit up his eyes. He loved his family, she thought. She couldn't help smiling back at him.

"She's eleven months older than I am and thinks she can boss me around."

"Not many people can do that because of your arrogant attitude."

"Arrogant?"

"Um…I think you know what I mean," she said, blushing a little because she'd never meant to say that out loud.

"I really do not know. Explain it to me."

She shook her. "I'm not myself today. I didn't mean to say that."

Tristan tucked a loose strand of her hair behind her ear. She tried not to react to his touch. But everything feminine in her came to attention. She almost sighed, but that would have been too revealing. So instead she took a deep breath.

"Looks like she does a fairly good job at it. Bossing you around that is," Sheri said.

"Well, she is not the only one," Tristan said, arching one eyebrow at her as he led her across the tarmac toward the waiting car.

"I would never try to boss you around," she said.

"I might let you in bed," he said, and they were at Blanche's side before she could respond.

"Blanche, this is Sheri Donnelly. Sheri this is my sister, Blanche Sabina-Christophe."

Sheri held her hand out to the other woman but Blanche leaned forward and air-kissed her cheek. Sheri did the same but felt kind of silly. Blanche smiled kindly at her.

"Your name is familiar to me. Have we met before?"

"She works for me in the New York office," Tristan said.

Blanche's eyes narrowed as she glared up at Tristan. Sheri took a step back as the affable woman of just seconds before was replaced by someone who definitely resembled Tristan when he was angry.

"I don't think we've had the chance to meet before, Mrs. Sabina-Christophe."

"Please, call me Blanche."

Sheri nodded. There was renewed tension between brother and sister and she had no idea what to say to break it. As Tristan's assistant she was used to stepping in and smoothing over awkward situations but this…there was no way she could interfere.

"Um…I guess you saw the tabloids."

"*Oui.* The entire family is gathering to discuss it."

Sheri took a step backward, longing to hide back on the jet. Even more, she yearned for her small, comforting brownstone. The one place in the world that had always been her constant. The one place in the world where she felt safe.

"Can you give us a moment, Blanche?"

"Certainly."

"Why don't Blanche and I take the second car

and give you and Sheri some time alone on the drive to your parents' house?" Gui said.

"I need to talk to Tristan about some family business," Blanche said.

"I don't mind riding with Gui," Sheri said, thinking that would be the easiest solution.

"I would mind. Blanche can go with him. We need to talk."

Sheri realized that his indulgent attitude toward his sister only lasted for so long. The commanding man Tristan normally was had come back to the surface.

"Tristan—"

"Blanche, this is not open to discussion."

She shrugged in a way that Sheri thought was distinctly French and turned to Gui. "I suppose that will be fine. You must be on your best behavior, Gui."

He lifted Blanche's hand to his mouth and brushed his lips across the back. "With you that will be easy."

"I'd be flattered if I didn't know you were always trying to charm anyone female."

Gui laughed and said, "You always say the nicest things."

"Your ego can stand it."

"Indeed," Gui said, leading her away.

Tristan led Sheri to the car, and she slid inside.

She started to move across the seat to make room for him, but he closed the door behind her and walked around toward the other side. She sat there for a moment feeling as if she'd stepped into someone else's life. And realized that she wanted it.

Tristan wasn't sure that coming to Paris was the best idea he'd ever had. But he needed the resources of his family and he'd wanted to take Sheri to the safest place he could think of. The Sabina house on the outskirts of Paris was just that.

His *grandmère* had been a famous actress in Europe, and his *grandpère,* a director twenty years her senior. They'd had a scandalous love affair that had resulted in a marriage that lasted for fifty years, until his *grandpère's* death. And the paparazzi had hounded them all their lives.

Tristan's mother had grown up with the photographers following her and the world being interested in everything she did. Tristan and his siblings had done the same.

They were used to the attention, but there were times like this when he resented it.

"Are you okay?" Tristan asked, looking at Sheri.

She'd be so easy to care for. Hell, he already cared more for her than he should. But he had to keep his focus, his distance from her, because he knew that she was barely holding herself together and a full-blown affair with him wasn't going to help her.

"I'm fine," she said, but she was clutching her purse to her stomach and staring out the window.

"Sheri, look at me."

"Not now, Tristan."

"Yes, now."

She shook her head and turned her body away from his as if to emphasize her determination.

He simply took her chin in his hand and turned her toward him. She had that wounded look in her big doe eyes again and he felt the impact all the way to his cold and lonely heart. She kept her gaze fixed at his chest.

"What is wrong now?"

"Um…I work for you. Everyone in the world knows I slept with you. Figure it out."

He bit the inside of his cheek to keep from smiling. There was the sassy girl he knew. The one that he'd been attracted to and hadn't understood why.

But now it all made sense. There was a real fire and passion in Sheri that she kept deeply buried.

"What happens between us is our business, *ma petite*."

"That's easy for you to say. Guys will slap you on the back and say, go, you. But everyone will look at me and think…"

"Sheri, please look at me."

She turned to face him fully and lifted those beautiful brown eyes of hers to meet his gaze.

"You are never going to be able to control what anyone thinks about you but you can control how you feel about what happened. Do you regret becoming my lover?" he asked.

She nibbled her lower lip and then sighed. "No. I don't. Being in your arms was incredible."

"Then don't worry about the photos or the press or any of it."

She arched one eyebrow at him. "That'd be a little easier to do if I hadn't met that lot head-on this morning. It was a little scary."

"It is irritating. I will install you at my parents' house and then take care of the paparazzi."

"You keep saying that. And I don't like it."

"What don't you like?"

"You taking care of everything. I'm not some doormat. Despite how I might act at the office."

"You're borderline insubordinate at the office." He smiled to show that he was joking.

"Only borderline? I'll have to work on that," she

said, and he saw the spark of her personality peeking through the sadness that had engulfed her for most of the day.

He knew it was a mistake to want to cheer her up. To care so much about her happiness, and about seeing her smile, but he did. He wasn't going to be able to offer her anything else, so his protection and her happiness were it.

"I'm not above using discipline to keep you in line."

"Like what? You going to spank me?" She shook her head and covered her mouth with her hands. "I can't believe I said that."

Immediately he had a vivid image of her sweet, bare ass as she lay over his lap. He hardened, then shifted to relieve some of the pressure at his inseam.

She flushed, and he knew that he wasn't going to be able to keep his hands off her. He wanted her again. If he'd been able to distance himself in Mykonos, take her to the airport and put her on a commercial flight, it would have been different but now…he was going to have her again.

He needed to get her out of his system.

Seven

As her words echoed between them, Tristan leaned forward, took her face in both of his hands and kissed her. She closed her eyes and surrendered to the feelings he drew from her effortlessly. She'd been craving this for so long. It felt as if a lifetime had passed, instead of just hours, since he'd touched her like this.

She opened her mouth for his tongue, which teased hers. He ran it along the roof of her mouth and then drew back, catching her lower lip between his teeth and suckling her.

She shifted closer to him on the seat, needing more of him. Shivers of desire coursed through her body. She put her hands on his face, touched his jaw and then slid her fingers into his hair.

It was thick and silky. She tilted her head to the side and he drew her even closer to him as his mouth continued to explore hers.

He drew back from her and she opened her eyes, staring up at him. "I can't get enough of you," he said.

"Is that a bad thing?" she asked. Her lips were tingling from the contact with his.

"Of course not. I am French. We live for physical love."

"And romantic love?" she asked, because she knew deep inside that she was falling in love with him. The seeds had been planted long before she'd known him as anything other than an attractive man who was her boss.

"Romantic love...what about it, Sheri?"

"Do you believe in it, or just lust?"

"I believe that we all get a once-in-a-lifetime chance at romantic love."

"Once in a lifetime?" she asked. That sounded good to her. "I believe in that, too."

He gave her a little half smile. She thought about what she knew of Tristan. How he was rumored to still be mourning his deceased wife even though she'd been gone for a long time.

"Did you— Never mind."

"Go ahead and ask."

She knew she was prying, but after all they'd shared, and given the fact that she was vulnerable to Tristan in a way she'd tried to not let herself be to any man, she had to ask.

"Did you have that with your wife?"

He looked at her then, and the expression in his eyes made her realize there were layers to Tristan she might never understand. The pain in his eyes took her breath away.

"Yes."

She nodded. There really wasn't anything else to say. His one-word answer in that monotone told her everything she wanted to know about where this relationship was heading. Ha, she was kidding herself to call it a relationship. It was a one-night stand, except…he'd just kissed her like he wanted her again.

So she had to decide right now. Was she going to be an affair for him? Could she really deny herself Tristan just because he couldn't love her?

"Have you ever experienced that?" he asked her.

"Would I be here if I had?" she asked, careful

not to let on that she suspected he could be that once-in-a-lifetime love for her.

"I guess not," he said, stroking his finger down the side of her face and then down the length of her neck. "Why haven't you?"

She swallowed hard. "I don't know. I don't trust easily."

"But you trust me," he said. "You came to my bed last night."

"It wasn't easy," she said. "But you wanted me…."

"And you wanted me, too."

"Yes, I did."

"Did? And now you do not?" he asked. He traced the scoop neck of her blouse and then moved his fingertip lower, to the upper curve of her breast.

She shifted her shoulders and had to force herself not to follow his touch when he pulled his hand away.

"Do you still want me, *ma petite?*"

"You know I do. One night…it doesn't seem like enough time with you."

"What would be enough time?" he asked.

She doubted a lifetime would be, but she couldn't say that. So instead she shrugged.

He smiled down at her. "I want more time with

you. Are you willing to continue what we started last night?"

She thought about that. Her first instinct was to say yes. But what would that be like? Hell, she was going to be miserable when things ended between them anyway. Now or later…and later sounded much better than now. So…

"Yes."

He smiled at her. "Good."

"You are *so* arrogant."

"You say that as if it is a bad thing."

He leaned over and kissed her so deeply that she knew she'd made the right decision. Tristan might think all he had to offer her was lust but she sensed so much more swirling under the surface.

And he'd stayed, she thought, as she wrapped her arms around those broad shoulders of his and hugged him as close to her as she dared. She wanted to hold him even tighter, but she didn't, afraid he'd realize how much he meant to her. That might be the trigger that finally made him leave.

Rene waited for them under the portico at the side entrance of his parents' mansion. Tristan took one look at his older brother's face and knew that he was facing a long afternoon. And he also knew it was nothing that Sheri needed to be a part of.

His family was overbearing at the best of times. Today, with his face once again splashed on the pages of every gossip magazine, it would be even worse.

"You have two choices," he said, turning to Sheri as the car came to a stop. To the driver he called, "We need a minute, Tollerman, before we'll be getting out."

"Yes, sir."

Tristan curved his arm around Sheri's shoulders and drew her close to him.

"What are my choices?"

"I can have Tollerman take you to the Ritz and you can use the suite I keep there, but there is a chance that the paparazzi will be there."

"For me?"

"No. They wait there for a chance photo of anyone of interest. And I can call and ensure that you have security and can go in the back entrance."

"What's my other choice?" she asked.

"Come inside with me and sit by the pool while I deal with my family."

She sighed. "I'll stay with you."

"Good." He smiled at that. "We're ready now, Tollerman."

"Very well, sir."

The driver got out and opened Sheri's door first. As she slid out of the car, he noticed the way the fabric of her trousers pulled tight across the curves of her butt. The image of her across his lap flashed through his mind again. Dammit, he wasn't into anything kinky as a matter of routine, but he couldn't get the idea of spanking Sheri out of his head.

She glanced back at him just before the door closed and he realized she'd caught him staring. He rubbed his hand against his thigh and she giggled a little. He knew her thoughts were along the same line as his. That she'd found humor now made him feel good.

He climbed out of the car as Sheri came around to his side.

Rene pounced. "It's about time. We need to talk before you go inside."

"Blanche already delivered the news."

"Tristan—"

"Not now. Sheri, this is my brother, Rene."

She held out her right hand and wrapped her left arm around her own waist, something he noticed she did when she felt insecure. He didn't have to be a mind reader to tell that she felt vulnerable now.

It compounded his desire to make her safe. To take care of her. He was good at taking care of people, he thought. He didn't have to love her, but he could make love to her and take care of her until this storm blew over.

"*Enchanté*, Mademoiselle Donnelly. It's a pleasure to meet you in person."

"For me, too, Monsieur Sabina. Please call me Sheri."

"And I am Rene."

Tristan led her up the stairs away from his brother. He sensed she regretted saying she'd stay with him. He didn't give her a chance to change her mind, just ushered her into the house and found one of the downstairs maids.

"Nathalie, please escort Mademoiselle Donnelly to the pool area," he said in French.

"*Oui, monsieur.*"

"There's a cabana stocked with leisure clothing. I'll be a while, so you should eat lunch. Just tell Nathalie what you would like."

She glanced around the large foyer where Rene stood waiting for him and then she took his wrist and drew him aside. "Look," she said. "I think I've changed my mind about sitting by the pool."

"Too late."

"We're not at work. You can't just give orders and expect me to do what you say."

"Yes, I can. And I have. Go relax by the pool while I sort out my family."

"I don't like taking orders in my personal life."

"Too late. I'm a bossy kind of man, which you already know."

"Yes, but I thought—"

He bent and kissed her, because he knew Sheri would keep arguing and he needed to get her somewhere safe before Blanche and the rest of the family came out and started questioning him in front of her.

If he was going to protect her, he needed her safely tucked away.

He lifted his head, turned her toward Nathalie. "Go." He followed his command with a smack on her backside. She gave him a quick glance over her shoulder. "I will now, but this is the last time I'm going to be tucked away while you deal with a problem."

"We can discuss it the next time we're in this situation," he said, fairly confident that they'd never be in this situation again.

She shook her head, and he wondered if she regretted going with him last night. He watched her walk away, trying to make himself regret that he'd taken a nice young woman and put her in this situation, but he couldn't. There was something about Sheri that drew him. For safety's sake, he should back away, but he'd always lived for danger and this woman seemed like a challenge he could handle.

"An employee! Tristan, honestly, you've gone too far this time."

"Rene, it's not as it seems."

"Good luck explaining that to the board."

Tristan felt very much the wayward son as he leaned against the mantel in his father's den. It was funny to him that, outside of this room, he was considered to be a forceful man. Inside, he was always keenly aware that he was his father's son. And that he'd never lived up to the expectations Louis had for sons. Rene did it exceptionally well but he'd been the eldest and the expectations for him had been different than the expectations for Tristan, which were pretty much that he simply stayed out of trouble.

"This can't continue," his mother said.

"Maman, it's not as if I seek out this kind of publicity."

"We know that, Tris. But you have to admit your behavior is out of control," Blanche said.

"Out of control? I'm trying to have a normal life."

"We want you to settle down," his father said. "That's the only real solution to this problem. Until you do, the paparazzi aren't going to lose interest in you."

Tristan shrugged one shoulder. He wasn't marrying again, something he'd promised to Cecile on her deathbed. Their relationship had been so intense, even in those last moments when he'd held her fragile body in his arms and watched her slowly slip away from him.

"The press have always been interested in our family," he said.

"The rest of us don't do anything that gives them a reason to photograph us," Rene said.

"What are you getting at? I can't control their actions."

"That's right, you can hardly control your own," his father said.

"*Père,* I'm grown. I don't answer to you."

"Do you answer to Ms. Donnelly?" Blanche quietly interjected into what would have been a very heated argument between him and his father.

"Why do you ask?" Protecting Sheri had been on his mind since she'd screamed outside the villa on Mykonos. He'd brought her here thinking that together the entire Sabina family could help him keep her out of the glare of the spotlight, but he realized now that he didn't want to leave her in their care. Not that the option of doing that was open to him now.

"Because she's not used to being followed by tabloid photographers, and she works for us."

"Tristan, you slept with an *employee?*" his mother asked.

"Enough. I'm not discussing my personal life with any of you."

"This isn't personal. It's business."

"How do you figure, Rene?"

"If it involves someone who works for the Sabina Group, that does involve us. She's not some heiress used to the paparazzi and she would never have been exposed to them if not for Tristan," Rene said.

"I agree. We're going to have to do something. Maybe transfer her to the London office," Louis said.

"We're not transferring her anywhere. She's always lived in Brooklyn and I don't want her life disrupted," Tristan said.

"It's a little late for that," Blanche said.

Everyone joined in the discussion on what should be done with Sheri and how Tristan should have shown more sense, and he shook his head. He was tempted to grab Sheri and leave. Just walk away from his family and his position at Sabina Group, but he liked the magazine he'd started. And he wasn't a quitter. Never had been, even when the odds were stacked against him.

So he pushed away from the fireplace and waited until everyone stopped talking at once.

"Sheri isn't your concern, Rene."

"How do you figure?"

"She's my fiancée, so I'll be the one to look after her." The words came out of nowhere and stunned everyone into silence. He heard his mother gasp, and Blanche's expression—a cross between disbelief and shock—was comical.

"Fiancée? You're going to marry this girl?"

He felt trapped by circumstances and his own desires. He wanted Sheri and wasn't ready to let her go just yet. But he knew he had to do something to protect her from the tabloid press. As his fiancée, she'd be in the society pages for the right reasons.

He rubbed the back of his neck as he thought of the last time he'd told his family he was getting married. Cecile had been standing at his side, but otherwise the stunned disbelief of his family was exactly the same.

He tried to find the humor in it, but it was difficult. "Now that everything is settled about Mademoiselle Donnelly, I'm going to my townhome in Paris."

"Everything isn't settled, Tristan. Bring your fiancée in here so we can all toast the new couple," Rene said.

"And I want to talk to her about planning a party," Blanche said. "We can do it in conjunction with the launch of our summer fashion guide. I think that will be the best way to introduce her properly to the world at large and as one of us, don't you think?"

Tristan shook his head. "She doesn't have time to plan a party. She's my assistant."

"Nonsense, Tris, she's your fiancée now, that takes precedence."

"No, Blanche, it doesn't. You and Maman can plan a party for us if you want to, but Sheri will continue working for me."

"Why?"

"Because that is her desire. That's the reason we've kept our engagement secret all this time."

Eight

Sheri had changed into a red-and-white maillot and a wraparound sarong. She sat in the dappled sunlight that filtered into the glass-enclosed pool. There was a sense of peace that reminded her of the quietness of her own small backyard garden in Brooklyn, although the indoor pool was heavily landscaped and looked like paradise, while her own garden was little more than a few fruit trees, bare now that it was the middle of February.

Aunt Millie had been a big believer that being

outside could soothe the soul as nothing else could. When Sheri had been upset by her father once again missing a birthday or scheduled visit, Aunt Millie would lead her to the backyard and tell her stories of fairy princesses who lived in the garden under Sheri's bedroom window.

She closed her eyes, reaching out with her mind to her aunt. She wished she could feel Millie's arms around her once again. She was so tired of being alone. Of facing every situation on her own.

She heard the sound of footsteps and glanced over her shoulder as Tristan approached. He looked grim, and she wondered if the paparazzi had followed them and were now camped out on his parents' doorstep.

She stood up. "Is something wrong?"

He shook his head. "Sit down."

She sank back down onto the lounge chair. It was thickly cushioned, probably more comfortable than the old mattress she slept on at home.

"What's up?"

"I've decided the best way to handle the paparazzi is to take charge of the situation."

She liked the sound of that. "Good. Running away seems cowardly to me."

He gave her a faint smile. "You never fail to

amaze me," he said, and for once that arrogant tone she associated with him wasn't there.

"How am I doing that?" She usually glided through life being dependable or invisible. Which, she realized, was why the photographers had shaken her. She'd never stood out from the people she worked with or dealt with on a daily basis. How could she handle the attention of the world?

"By being calm about the photographers and my family. A quick flight out of Greece to Paris hasn't seemed to upset you at all."

It was sweet of Tristan to say that, but she was anything but calm. "I guess we're going to pretend that moment at the airport where I almost bolted didn't happen. And the time when I started screaming in front of the photographers," she said in a teasing tone.

That startled a laugh out of him, and she felt better for it.

"*Exactly.* The solution I propose may sound a bit odd to you at first. But let me explain everything before you comment on it."

"Okay," she said, taking a deep breath. What was he going to say? Well, what could he say? *The board and I think you need to find a new job. And I want you to deny ever being with me.*

His touch on her shoulder startled her out of her thoughts and she looked up into those deep gray eyes of his. She loved his eyes, and had often imagined him looking at her just as he was right now.

"Breathe," he said.

"I am," she said, with a long exhale.

He took her hand in his and held it loosely in his grip. "You have such pretty hands."

Of course he'd notice her hands. Considering she wasn't beautiful like the women he normally surrounded himself with, her hands were probably the only thing he'd found good-looking about her.

He lifted one of them to his mouth and kissed the back of it, then tucked his fingers around it. She smiled at the way he did it…linking them together.

She felt a bit of calm steal over her. This didn't feel like the big brush-off. And she'd had enough experience with being shown the door that she'd know if a man was doing that to her.

In fact, her stomach wasn't a tight knot like it had been the day that her father had sat her down to talk. She realized suddenly that her dreams were still alive. All this time, she'd thought she was a cynic and a realist but, sitting in this beautiful solarium filled with the sound from the waterfall at the end of the pool and the scents of Eden around her, she was holding her breath not because she felt like something bad was about to happen, but because she anticipated something good.

Tristan made her feel like the kind of woman for whom a man would make a grand gesture to keep in his life. And in the car, he'd all but said he wanted to continue their affair. So what could this be about? What was he going to say to her now, in this paradise?

"So what did you come up with?"

"I want you to be my fiancée," he said.

Sheri was sure she'd misunderstood him, because she knew he wasn't the marrying kind, but she thought he'd said *be his fiancée*.

"What?"

"I want you to be my fiancée for the time being. Just until the furor of the press dies down."

She felt the blood rush from her face and closed her eyes. Of course, it was temporary. She had forgotten the one truth of her life—she was meant to be alone.

Sheri pulled away from him and got to her feet. Moving a few yards away, she wrapped one arm around her waist and then a few seconds later turned back to him, putting both hands on her hips.

"Why would I agree to that? That's a crazy solution. Who's going to care that we're engaged?"

"The Sabina Group board, for one. They wanted to transfer you to the London office where you could hide out until this blows over."

"Why wouldn't that work?"

"Because I need you in the New York office," he said. He wasn't giving her up. She was one of the only two assistants he'd ever had that didn't annoy him and actually made him want to go into the office, Lucille being the other.

"I'm still not following why you came up with this solution," she said. She wasn't belligerent or demanding, which he would have brushed aside.

"The only thing that will get the press off your back is if we take control of what they are covering. A wedding is the kind of thing they eat up."

She tipped her head to the side and gave him a long, level stare. "So, we're getting married?"

"No, just planning a wedding."

She shook her head. "Do I seem that desperate to you?"

"No, you don't seem desperate."

"Well, then why do you think I'd settle for being your pretend fiancée?"

"Because you aren't going to be able to stay here at my parents' house the way I'd hoped. And your home in Brooklyn isn't going to offer you any protection from the paparazzi. They'll follow you from the second you leave until the moment you return. Are you ready to deal with that on your own?"

She shook her head and then turned away from him. He let her have a moment of privacy, but he could sense her weakening and he'd already decided this was best for both of them.

And he wasn't backing down. Sheri was going to be standing in his parents' den really soon, toasting their engagement with a smile that would convince the world that they were the real deal.

He went over to her, touching her shoulders. How he'd never noticed her before last night still amazed him. She had an incredible body. He lowered his head, dropping a soft nibbling kiss against the back of her neck. He ran his hands down her arms and drew her back against his body.

"I want what's best for you, *ma petite*," he said, unable to resist kissing her collarbone.

Her skin tasted faintly sweet, something he'd never noticed in a woman before. But she tasted good to him. And he brushed his tongue against her smooth skin to take a little more of that taste into his mouth.

She shivered in his arms, arching against him, tipping her head back against his shoulder. Her eyes were wide as she looked up at him. So very wide and vulnerable.

Her mouth trembled and he knew she was on the cusp of giving in to him. He leaned down and kissed her. Not softly, but with all the passion inside of him. He kissed her like a man who was hungry for his woman and wanted everything that she had to give.

He broke the kiss only when he needed to breathe and immediately came back to her again, sucking her lower lip into his mouth and drawing on it. She moaned and turned in his arms until he felt the curve of her breast brush his upper arm. Her nipple was hard; he felt it through the fabric of her maillot.

He felt a twinge of conscience at pushing her now. But in the end, he knew what he had to do to take care of her. This was all that was in his control.

"Tristan?"

"Hmm?"

"I… Why don't you want to really marry me?" she asked, her voice so soft it was hardly a whisper.

He closed his own eyes. "I told you I had my once-in-a-lifetime love, remember?"

"Yes, of course I do. But what has that got to do with marriage?"

Tristan turned her in his arms and tucked her up close to his body, trying not to remember how perfectly they'd fit together when making love despite the differences in their heights. Once he'd been buried hilt-deep in her body, he'd felt the perfection of it.

He drew her back into his arms, lowering his head once more, wanting to take her mouth and stop her questions.

But she pulled away. "No more. I want you, but I want answers, too. I don't understand why you won't really marry me."

"It is not you," he said, the words spilling out. "I will never marry again."

"Then why pretend to be engaged?"

He pushed his hands through his hair and turned his back on her. He couldn't look at her and lie. When she'd said she couldn't lie to him, in the office a few short weeks ago, he'd had no idea what she felt like. Now he did.

And he wasn't giving her up. He hadn't gotten Sheri Donnelly out of his system yet and he wasn't going to let her go until he did.

"It's the only way I can protect you the way I want to, *ma petite.*"

"Why do I need protecting?"

"Because this is my world and I seduced you without thinking of the consequences."

"You didn't force me to sleep with you," she said, cheeky tone in place.

"I know that, Sheri. But you weren't aware of what it is like to be hounded by the press and I should have taken steps to protect you and your identity from them."

Even if she'd known how things would turn out this morning, Sheri doubted that she would have not gone with Tristan last night. Even now, sitting in a well-appointed formal living room surrounded by the entire Sabina family, she didn't regret her decision.

Tristan sat next to her, his arm resting casually over her shoulders. He toyed with her hair, something he did a lot. Sitting there she felt a sense of rightness all the way to her soul and she knew she'd said yes to his outrageous proposal for one reason and one reason alone. She was going to find a way to make Tristan Sabina fall in love with her.

She was going to do everything in her power to keep this man who'd stayed. And she was coming to realize that Tristan gave her clues all the time about what it was that he enjoyed about her.

If she paid attention, she could be what he needed her to be for him to fall in love with her. It didn't have to be the all-encompassing love that he'd had with his late wife. She'd be satisfied with just some kind of deep caring from him.

She settled into the curve of his body as Rene lifted his champagne flute and said something in French that she couldn't understand. Tristan squeezed her shoulder and lifted his own flute. So she did the same, taking a delicate sip of the delicious French sparkling wine.

Tristan leaned closer to Sheri and whispered directly in her ear. "Rene said that he wishes us happiness and laughter all the days of our lives."

She smiled up at him. "Well, I want that, too."

Tristan's eyes narrowed a bit but he dropped a quick kiss on her nose. She realized that he was going to fight her the entire time. Try to keep her in the role of pretend fiancée. And the only way she was going to get him to think of her as anything else was to make him need her.

He needed her body, but was sex enough? Could she hold him with sex when she'd never really tried to keep any of her previous lovers...? Okay, there hadn't been that many, but she had to look at it from a historical perspective.

Blanche stood up next. Tristan's sister made Lucille look like a country bumpkin. She was simply elegant and sophisticated. She spoke in a sweet tone, smiling indulgently toward Tristan.

Again the toast was in French. Tristan didn't lift his glass this time. Instead he put it on the table and stood up, leaving the room without a comment.

Sheri felt awkward. "I'm sorry, my French isn't good enough to know what you said."

Blanche shook her head. "I just said that we were happy to see him moving past the pain of heartache and moving into a new love."

But the way they were all staring at her, she realized they knew what she'd known all along. That Tristan wasn't in love with her. It was fine for the two of them to know that lust was all they had between them. But his family...

"I'm not the love of his life," she said.

"I'm not so sure about that, Sheri. You're the first woman he's brought to meet us in eight years."

Sheri took small comfort in that. "Will you please excuse me?"

"Of course. If you are looking for Tristan, try the third floor. Fourth door on the left."

She left the room without another word. Walking slowly through the house, she was reminded again that there was a huge difference between her and Tristan. This one—the material things—didn't seem as big a deal as their difference in willingness to love.

Tristan was such a dominant, arrogant man, she had a hard time imagining that he was afraid of anything, especially falling in love again.

But those rumors about his first marriage... about his first wife... She needed to find out exactly what she was up against.

She climbed the curving staircase, looking at the huge portraits hung on the walls. Pictures of men who resembled Tristan, and some portraits of people who were vaguely familiar to her. His famous grandparents, she thought.

He'd grown up surrounded by a rich history, whereas she had only what she took with her. Aunt

Millie's warm memory and the cold emptiness of her father's desertion.

She got to the third floor. At the landing there was an upholstered chaise centered under a dominant portrait of the Sabina siblings when they were younger…probably late teens, she thought.

Blanche was seated in the center and Rene and Tristan stood on either side of her. Blanche was elegant even as a teenager, smiling beguilingly out of the portrait. Rene was serious and even then looked as if he were all business. And Tristan. Her heart caught in her throat. He was laughing, very much the rebel in his casual rock T-shirt, whereas his siblings were dressed to the nines.

She had never seen an expression like that on Tristan's face and she thought that this is the part of him that died when his wife did.

She reached out to touch his face, letting her fingers hover over the curve of his mouth. It felt like what she'd done so many times in her apartment late at night. Lusting after a man she couldn't have.

And now that she had the Tristan she'd thought she wanted, she realized he only was giving her half of himself. The part he thought she'd accept without question.

And she knew now she wanted more. She was

falling in love with Tristan Sabina, and she wasn't going to be satisfied with merely keeping him from leaving.

She needed him to fall in love with her. Not just to care for her, but really fall head over heels in love. She turned to walk down the hall and saw the gilt-framed mirror and the reflection of the woman there.

She was going to have to make some serious changes if she was going to win Tristan's love.

Nine

Two weeks later, Sheri wasn't sure who she was anymore. Despite the fact that Tristan wanted their lives to remain the same, they had been changed by the "engagement." Blanche had even taken her shopping before allowing her to leave Paris. And Sheri had enjoyed her time with Blanche.

She found herself interested in clothing for the very first time. Standing in front of her closet in the brownstone in Brooklyn, she realized that it might be a bit small. It never had been before.

But then, she'd never had a closet full of outfits

for every type of event known to man. She'd turned into a socialite without even trying. She was exhausted, because Tristan had been extremely serious when he said that he still wanted her to work for him.

Her phone rang while she was in the middle of getting dressed in a Chanel linen-and-cashmere strip tunic that ended well above her knees, showing off her trim calves and ankles. She'd never really thought about her body, but Tristan's lovemaking and comments left no doubt that he liked hers. Her legs were slim because she'd always lived in the city and walked everywhere.

"Hello?"

She was getting better at accessorizing, but had been keeping the outfits put together the way Blanche had arranged them for her. Trying to make Tristan fall in love with her, trying to remember how to be fashionable and avoiding the paparazzi were a lot to add to her life. Most of the time she felt as if she was juggling and dropping most of the balls.

"*Bonjour, ma petite.* I'm downstairs in the car waiting for you."

"Good morning, Tristan. I'm almost ready."

Propping the phone between her ear and shoulder, she paired the tunic dress with a pair of lizard-

and-lambskin sandals and a calf-skin belt in white with a distinctive Chanel belt buckle. She had a chunky bracelet that she put on her right arm and then she carefully opened the box with the diamond watch that Tristan's parents had given her as an engagement present. They'd had her initials and the date of their engagement—the date she and Tristan had made up—engraved on the back.

"This would be a lot easier if you'd just move in with me."

"No, it wouldn't."

"Why wouldn't it?"

"Because then I'd have to move out again when the engagement was over. This way, I'll never have lived in your house."

"Or slept in my bed for an entire night," he said.

She always came back home after they made love at his apartment. And he never stayed the night at her place. She was doing everything she could to insulate herself against the pain of heartbreak, but she had the feeling that no matter what she did, it was still going to hurt her if he left.

"Well…"

"Well, what? Why are you so stubborn about this one thing?"

"Because I'm your pretend fiancée, Tristan. If

I were really your woman and you were going to claim me in front of the world, then I'd be living with you in a heartbeat."

He said nothing, as she'd suspected he would. "I'll be down in a minute."

She hung up the phone and turned back to the mirror. Her dark brown hair now had highlights and she knew how to put on makeup so that she looked like all the other women who had always surrounded Tristan. A part of her was amazed at how she looked, another part disgusted. She was changing every part of herself for a man who was her *pretend* fiancé, and she was no closer to figuring out how to make him fall in love with her.

She stared down at the engagement ring on her left hand. Tristan had wanted something big and flashy but she'd stubbornly refused. If he really loved her and was buying her a ring that symbolized his love, she would have bowed to his wishes, but he'd been buying the ring for others to see and she had dug in her heels.

She liked the understated platinum ring she had on. It fit her hand and her finger. And unlike a more costly ring, it didn't make her feel as if she'd sold herself to Tristan.

The clothes she knew she'd donate to Dress

for Success when she was done pretending to be his fiancée—if she didn't turn the pretend part into reality.

"Why did you hang up on me?"

She yelped and spun around. Tristan stood there, gorgeous as always. "Why are you in my house?"

"You gave me a key, remember? I am your fiancé."

She made a face at him in the mirror. "Just for pretend."

"Sheri."

He said her name in a stern tone that told her she was pushing too hard. But she didn't want to back down. She was tired of pretending, and the only way for that to stop was for Tristan to see her as more than a lover and an assistant. She was pretty sure that's all he saw when he looked at her.

"What?"

"What is the matter with you this morning?"

She shrugged. If he'd demanded an answer or kept pushing her, she could have gotten angry and then used her anger to keep the truth at bay.

"Answer me. Please."

"No."

She reached for a pair of platinum bangle earrings and slipped them into her ears. Tristan came up behind her, rested his hands on her shoulders and leaned in low so that his gaze met hers in the mirror.

"What is wrong?"

She bit her lower lip, afraid of saying too much. But suddenly she realized that the changes she made were all superficial and deep inside she was the woman she'd always been. And that woman wanted more.

"I don't want to be your fake fiancée. And frankly, I can't understand why this isn't real."

Tristan would be damned if he was going to have this conversation with her. He'd been dodging the same questions from Gui, who had warned him that toying with a woman's emotions was only going to lead to trouble. And Christos, who didn't know the engagement wasn't real and thought that he had made a great decision. Since Christos's marriage to Ava, the man thought all anyone needed to be happy was a wife.

But Tristan knew better. He wasn't toying with Sheri's emotions, and he sure as hell wasn't going to really marry her. He knew himself well enough to know that there were only certain things he could control. And surprisingly Sheri was one of them.

He bent his head to nibble on her neck in the spot he knew was sensitive. She undulated under his hands and reached back to put her arms around his neck, turning her head to the side until their lips met.

He hated not waking up with her every morning. He suspected that was why he still wasn't ready to move on from her. He had yet to spend an entire night with her, save for that first one on Mykonos. And he hadn't appreciated it then.

"I thought you were in a hurry this morning," she said, turning in his arms.

"Just to see you." Her dresser surface was clear except for a small jewelry box. "Are you wearing panties?"

"Yes," she said. "I tend to wear them when I'm going to work."

"Take them off."

"Ask me nicely," she said.

And Tristan leaned down to take her mouth with his, kissing her slowly, thoroughly. He caught her earlobe between his teeth and breathed into her ear as he said, "Please."

She shivered delicately, her hands clenching on his shoulders before she stepped back half an inch. "Okay."

She tugged the short hemline of her dress higher

and lowered a pair of whisper-thin white cotton panties. She balanced herself by putting one hand behind her on the dresser as she stepped out of her underpants.

The movement thrust her breasts forward. The high, round neck of her tunic didn't show nearly enough of her chest for him. He reached for the belt at her waist and unhooked it, letting it fall to the floor.

He lifted her up on top of the dresser and pushed her tunic dress to her waist. She parted her legs and he groaned her name. Blood rushed through his veins, pooling in his groin.

She continued smiling up at him as she leaned back on her elbows. "Was this what you had in mind?"

"Almost," he said, pushing her dress even higher until her breasts were bared to his gaze. The bra she wore had thin lacy cups and he could see the distended nipples peeking through the lace. He leaned down and licked them both.

Her legs shifted restlessly around his hips. Though it had been just last night, it felt like an eternity since he'd last held her in his arms.

He'd been aroused since he'd entered her house. She reached up and pulled his head down to hers. Her mouth opened under his and he told himself to take it slow, but slow wasn't in his programming with this woman. She was pure feminine temptation and he had her in his arms. He slid his hands down her back, finding the clasp of her bra and undoing it.

He grasped her buttocks, pulling her forward until he was pressed against her feminine mound. He felt the humid warmth at her center through the fabric of his pants and reached between them to caress her. She shifted more fully into him.

The fabric of her dress, bunched under her arms, just covered her breasts as she breathed heavily. He saw the hint of the rosy flesh of her nipples and lowered his head, using his teeth to pull the loosened fabric away from her skin. He ran the tip of one fingertip around her aroused flesh. She trembled in his arms.

Lowering his head he took one of her nipples in his mouth and suckled her. She held him to her with a strength that surprised him, but shouldn't have.

Her fingers drifted down his back and then slid around front to work open the buttons of his shirt. He growled deep in his throat when she leaned forward to brush kisses against his chest.

She licked and nibbled and made him feel like her plaything. He wanted to let her have her way with him, but there was no room here, no time for seduction or extended lovemaking.

He pulled her to him and lifted her slightly so that her nipples brushed his chest. Holding her carefully, he rotated his shoulders and rubbed against her. Blood roared in his ears. He was so hard, so full right now that he needed to be inside of her body.

He caressed her creamy thighs. God, she was soft. She moaned as he neared her center and then sighed when he brushed his fingertips across the entrance to her body.

The area was warm and wet. He slipped one finger into her and hesitated for a second, looking down into her eyes.

She bit down on her lower lip and he felt the minute movements of her hips as she tried to move his touch where she needed it.

He was beyond teasing her or prolonging anything. He needed her *now.* He swept her dress over her head and tossed it on the floor. She shrugged out of her bra and he lifted her off the dresser, turning her to face its mirror.

"What are you doing?" she asked, looking over her shoulder at him.

"I want you to watch us as I make love to you."

She murmured something he didn't catch. "Bend over slightly, *ma petite.*"

She did as he asked, her eyes watching his in the mirror. "Take your shirt off, please. I want to see your chest."

He smiled at her as he shrugged off the shirt she'd unbuttoned. His tie was tangled in the collar, but he managed to get them both off. He took out the condom he'd put in his pocket this morning and donned it quickly.

"Hold on and keep your eyes on mine in the mirror."

"Yes," she said.

He covered her with his body. Their naked loins pressed together and he shook under the impact.

He cupped her breasts in his hands then slipped one hand down her body, finding her wet and ready. He adjusted his stance, and then entered her with one long, hard stroke.

She moaned his name, still holding his gaze. He bit softly at her neck and felt the reaction all the way to his toes when she squirmed in his arms and thrust her hips back toward him.

A tingling started in the base of his spine and he knew his climax was close. She writhed more frantically in his arms and he moved deep with each stroke. Breathing out through his mouth, he tried to hold back the inevitable. He slid one hand down her abdomen, through the slick folds of her sex, finding her center. He circled that aroused bit of flesh then scraped it very carefully with his nail. She screamed his name and tightened around him. Tristan pulled one hand from her body and locked his fingers on the dresser over her small hand, then penetrated her as deeply as he could. Biting down on the back of her neck, he came long and hard.

Their eyes met again in the mirror and he knew that he wasn't going to find a way to live without her while he kept making love to her. And that meant he needed to come up with another plan. Something that didn't involve her being his pretend fiancée.

Ten

Two weeks later Sheri was still no closer to getting the answers she wanted from Tristan. But plans for the engagement party were going forward. The Paris branch of the Sabina Group was prepared to launch a new magazine on weddings and was using their engagement party as the first big glamorous event they'd cover. She'd promised Tristan that she'd stay with him until the engagement party was over.

A part of her worried that what she'd found with him was going to end too soon. Another part was afraid that it wouldn't end soon enough.

The one thing she didn't doubt was that she was in love with Tristan.

"Sheri, have Maurice come to my office in ten minutes."

"He's going to want to know what you need to see him about."

Tristan glanced up from the folder in his hands. "I'm going to fly your suggestion for the Travelogue column at the back. See if we can use celebrities instead of travel writers."

"Really? It was just an idea to boost readership."

"I know. I like it. I'll make sure that Maurice knows you came up with it."

She smiled. "I don't care about that."

Tristan leaned one hip against the side of her desk. "What do you care about?"

"World peace," she said, completely deadpan. She didn't want to have a serious discussion at work, but this was the only time when Tristan really opened up to her. It was almost as if he knew she'd only let things go so far in the office.

"*Ma petite,* are you going to leave me for a beauty pageant?"

"Not my scene."

"I know. This is your scene, isn't it?"

She nodded. "Working with you suits me to a tee."

"Just working?"

"Well, we don't live together."

"And whose fault is that?" He sounded almost huffy.

"Yours."

"Mine? I asked you to move in with me."

"More like ordered." She smiled. Take that.

"It didn't do me a lot of good."

"You wouldn't want a woman who just said yes to your every whim." That she knew.

"Try me."

"Try you? How?"

"Move in with me. Stop making me take you back to Brooklyn every night."

"What would change if I did that?" She was so tempted to say yes. Had been since the first time he'd told her to move in with him.

He leaned in close. "We'd be together all the time."

"But just temporarily."

"Is that what's stopping you from saying yes?"

She wasn't going to answer that question. She'd have to reveal too much of herself, too many things she'd long kept hidden. She glanced down at her computer screen and clicked on the instant messenger button to summon Maurice. The sooner they had someone else in the office, the better it would be for her.

"Sheri?"

"Hmm…"

"Look at me."

She glanced up.

"I want to know why you haven't moved in with me. The truth this time."

She folded her hands together on her desk blotter and then pulled them apart. "It is the temporary thing."

"I don't understand how it's any different if you move in with me," he said.

Sheri pushed her chair back from the desk and got up, walking around so that he wasn't leaning over her. "The difference is I've never lived anywhere but that brownstone."

Tristan stood up from where he'd been leaning against the desk. "The brownstone is your home."

"Yes. It's my home. It's the one constant I've had in my life since I was eight, when my mother died and my father dumped me at my aunt's, and, as you pointed out, what we've got going is only temporary."

Tristan didn't say anything else and Sheri wanted to curse at herself for letting the conversation get so personal. She really tried to be cool and breezy whenever she talked to him. Always tried so hard to keep her emotions bottled up and a secret from him.

"Is that it?"

"No…I'm also afraid that, if I move in with you, I'll start to buy in to the fantasy you've written for us. I might start to really believe that I'm your fiancée, and that would be devastating for me when you leave."

"All relationships end."

"How do you figure?"

"Even the strongest and most loving relationships end with death. So no matter what, everything is temporary."

"Tristan, that's sad."

"What is?"

"That you view life that way."

"It's realistic, Sheri. Hell, if you were to admit it, you see things the same way."

She shook her head. "No, I don't."

"Even though you won't leave your little brownstone?" he asked.

"That's different. I don't see relationships as temporary. I see them as unbalanced."

"I'm not following."

Sheri crossed her arms over her chest and stared at Tristan. His eyes were misty gray today because of the shirt he had on. He was so handsome, sometimes she worried that he'd wake up to the fact that there were a million gorgeous women in the world who'd gladly be his pretend fiancée and do whatever he asked of them.

"My reality and that brownstone are tied together. I see relationships as unbalanced because I've always been the one to care more than everyone else. And in the end, they've all left me behind."

Tristan didn't say anything and she felt like an idiot for revealing what she had.

"I'm going to run down and get Maurice."

She walked out of the office and down the hall, trying to pretend that nothing had changed, but knowing that everything had.

At the end of the day Tristan was tired. Sheri had made excuses to be away from her desk for most of the afternoon and he'd let her. There was work to do and he didn't need the distraction that she presented.

But in the back of his mind all he thought about was what she'd said about people leaving.

He thought in terms of temporary because his life had always been in constant change. The only thing he really counted on was his friendship with Gui and Christos.

And even that was changing, with Christos's marriage. He was happy for his friend, but at the same time concerned for him. Christos had never allowed himself to love a woman before, not the way he was in love with Ava. Tristan hoped they had a lifetime together, but his experience had taught him that they probably wouldn't.

There was a knock on his door.

"Enter."

The door opened to reveal Sheri. "I need your signature on these papers before I leave for the night."

She was all business. Until this afternoon, he hadn't realized how much of her personality she hid when she was in the office. It was only because of the last three weeks, when he'd seen so much more of her, that he now knew that.

She handed him a folder and he opened it up. He glanced at the papers and realized he wasn't reading them, so he closed the folder and pushed it aside.

"Please have a seat, Sheri."

"Is something wrong?"

"Yes. I have decided that I can't allow you to

continue living in Brooklyn. I have arranged for you to move into my place immediately."

She shook her head. "We've had this discussion."

"Exactly the problem. You need to be living with me." The engagement was working exactly as he'd hoped it would. The tabloid press was being very kind to Sheri and everyone he knew was excited for him. For the first time since Cecile had died, he felt as if his life was on the right path. He wasn't just running and trying to keep distance between himself and his life. And Sheri had given that to him.

And their conversation earlier had made him realize that he hadn't done the same for her. And that was not acceptable to him. Though he would never admit it, he liked the feelings she evoked in him. He knew they couldn't be love, because they felt nothing like the emotions he'd had for Cecile. But he did care for Sheri, and her happiness was important to him.

She nibbled on her lower lip. "What did I say that made you think that I'd agree to this?"

"It was what you did not say. Our engagement has given you a chance to change things about yourself. And I realized today that they were all surface changes. You need to move out of that brownstone if you are ever going to see yourself in a different light."

"Tristan—"

"No, listen to me. I know what it is like to be stuck in one place."

"That's a complete lie. You never stand still. How could you possibly know what I'm like?"

"That's precisely why I know. I have been always focused on the future to keep from dwelling on the past. Whereas you just stay there, stuck in time."

"I'm not sure you're qualified to be talking to me like this."

"Qualified?"

"Yes, qualified. You don't really know me all that well."

"I know you intimately, *ma petite.*"

"So did two other men and they didn't have a clue about what made me tick."

He hated the thought of anyone else having been with her. She was *his.* He didn't know exactly when he'd started thinking of her in those terms. But he did now. He wanted to tell her that he'd be the last man to know her intimately.

Where the hell had that thought come from?

"Those men weren't me. And I'm not taking no for an answer on this."

She stood up and walked over to him. She pushed her finger into his chest. "You're being a bully."

"No, I'm not. I'm being a man and taking charge."

"This is the twenty-first century, in case you'd forgotten. A time of compromise and 'working things out.' Women don't need a man to take charge," she said. The flash of temper in those big brown eyes of hers made him hard.

He was so tempted to lean down and kiss her. But she lifted her hand and put two fingers over his lips. "No, Tristan."

"No?"

"Don't kiss me, because then we'll be making love and I'll find myself living with you."

"I do not see the problem. You like making love with me, and you are going to be living with me either way."

She shook her head. "I don't want to live you."

"Give me one good reason why."

She wrapped her arms around her waist and took two steps back from him. "I…well, let me just say that I have a really good reason and leave it at that."

He crossed his arms over his chest and arched one eyebrow at her. "That might work if you had plied me with sex, but since you declined…I'm feeling stubborn."

She just stood there, and he wondered if he was pushing too hard. Why was this so important to him? He wasn't one hundred percent sure, but he guessed he wanted everything that Sheri had to give. She gave so willingly of her body, but she kept a tight rein on her soul. On the secrets that she guarded for herself. And he hated that there was a part of her that he didn't know. He wanted to know everything about her. He wanted to possess her completely.

"Tell me."

This had been the longest day of her life. And the most stressful. She had no idea what was going on with Tristan, not that she ever really had. She only knew that if he wanted to know what was inside her head, then they were both in trouble.

Tell me.

He wasn't asking nicely, he was demanding. And when it came to Tristan, she had absolutely no willpower. She wanted him to know her secrets because she loved him. Because no matter what her mind tried to tell her heart…her heart still believed that if he knew all her secrets, he'd fall for her, too.

Which was so stupid. He was the man who'd told her that all relationships were temporary. That all relationships ended. And heck, she knew that. Everyone she'd ever cared about was gone. Even Aunt Millie, through death, just as Tristan said. Though that's where she and Tristan differed. She knew the difference of having lived a life with someone you loved in it and having that person taken from you in death, versus having someone leave you because they couldn't love you.

"Why is it important to you? Why do you care?"

"Because I'm not the type of man who would let my fiancée live in another house. I would want her in my bed every night."

"You'd want *her* in your bed every night?" she asked.

"I want *you* in my bed every night. I want to wake up in the morning and see your face."

Suddenly Sheri wasn't sure what she knew anymore. Was Tristan simply afraid to admit his feelings for her? She knew he wanted her. No man had made love to her as often as he had. No man had ever said the things he did to her, whispering in her ear about how sexy she was and how much he wanted her.

But a part of her was afraid to believe it. She simply wasn't the kind of girl who inspired that feeling in a man like Tristan. Yet now, here he was, saying he wanted to wake up with her every morning and… "Tristan, I want that, too."

"Then why won't you move in?"

She looked at him. Just stared at the face that had graced the cover of more magazines than she'd ever dreamed of. And realized that at some point in time, he'd become so real to her. The Photoshopped perfection of those magazine photos wasn't the man she loved. *This* was the man she loved.

The man with a small scar under his left eye. And five-o'clock shadow on his jaw. The man who looked at her with exasperation at times, but always with honest emotion. Even if she couldn't always identify that emotion.

The man she loved.

"I haven't wanted to move in with you, because I love you, Tristan."

He took a step back. His arms fell from his chest and he looked at her as if she'd surprised him.

What had he expected?

"Should I not have said that?"

He shook his head. Then rubbed a hand over his forehead. "I was not expecting that."

"You weren't? Everyone knows how I feel about you."

Sheri felt so incredibly vulnerable right now.

She wrapped both arms around herself, holding herself as tightly as she could.

"Everyone?"

"Well, Ava noticed, and she hardly knows me at all. I'm pretty sure Lucille knows. She picked up on it the first time we spoke on the phone. Even your friend Gui knows. And I didn't have to tell him, either, he just guessed."

She didn't expect Tristan to love her back. Oh, man, what if that was what he was afraid of? "I don't expect you to love me."

He shook his head. "I don't believe in more than one love in a lifetime."

"I know that. I think that's part of the reason I love you so much. I want to fill up that emptiness you have."

Tristan walked over to her then. He took her shoulders in his hands and drew her toward him. His mouth came down on hers, heavy. He kissed her so deeply and with so much passion she couldn't help but respond.

She wrapped her arms around his shoulders and simply held on to him. He was in complete control and he made her forget everything. But she felt so much more now. It was as if, in admitting her love for him, she was finally free to let go of all the barriers she'd been keeping between them.

His tongue brushed hers and she moaned deep in her throat as shivers of awareness spread down her body. She moved closer to him. Needed to feel his body pressed up against hers.

Tristan lifted his head. "Thank you for loving me."

She couldn't help but smile at the polite way he said that. "You're welcome."

He brushed a strand of hair from her face and stared down at her with such seriousness that she felt a pang deep inside.

"There isn't a lack of love in my life, *ma petite*. There is a burned-out hole where my heart used to be, and I'm afraid no amount of love will ever bring it back."

Eleven

"I'm home," Tristan said as he walked into his apartment a little after ten o'clock one week later. He'd had a late dinner meeting and, for the first time since Cecile's death, he was coming home late not to servants and an empty house but to someone.

Sheri came down the hallway with a book in one hand and a pair of reading glasses on. She smiled at him. "How was it?"

"Not too bad. I think we will be launching a cooking magazine in the early fall next year."

"Good. I think that's great. Do you have any meetings you're going to need me to set up?"

"Yes, but I do not want to talk about that tonight."

Her smile turned suggestive. "What do you want to talk about then?"

"My woman."

"*Your* woman?"

She was sassing him and he had to admit he enjoyed it. He'd been unsure what living with Sheri would be like, but after the first night he'd realized that he made a good decision. He'd made love to Sheri twice last night, and then again in the morning before they'd left for work.

Having breakfast and then heading into the office together underscored to him what a great companion Sheri was. She suited his life perfectly. And the fact that she loved him made it all the sweeter.

"Were you waiting up?"

"Sort of."

"Why?"

She shrugged and he was starting to realize that's what she did when she didn't want to answer. It was her way of not lying about anything, of hiding when she felt that answering would leave her vulnerable.

"Will you come into the kitchen with me?" he

asked, shrugging out of his jacket. He hung it in the hall closet and then loosened his tie.

"Yes," she said. "Are you hungry? Mrs. Ranney made a pie."

His New York housekeeper was a whiz in the kitchen.

"Did you have any?" he asked, following her down the short hallway into the kitchen.

"No. I wasn't hungry earlier."

"Will you have a piece with me?"

"Maybe a small slice. I try not to eat after seven."

"Why?"

"Because unlike you, I don't work out every day."

"You could," he said, settling at the breakfast bar while Sheri moved around the kitchen. She found plates and cut them both a piece of pie. She was more at ease in his house than he was.

"You don't need to work out, *ma petite*. You look lovely as you are."

She arched one eyebrow at him. "Really?"

"Honestly. You have a sexy little body that I can't get enough of."

She blushed and smiled at him. "Then I should keep doing what I've been doing, and that's not eating late at night."

"Milk, coffee or some kind of after-dinner drink?"

She leaned over the breakfast bar to slide his plate in front of him. He took her chin in his hand and kissed her long and slow. Now he felt as if he was home. The home he found in her eyes and in her arms.

She pulled back, looking bemused, and he smiled inside. He loved that she was so guileless about how attractive she was and about the effect she had on him.

She turned away, grabbing a napkin and fork for him. "Did you want a drink?"

"Yes. Milk, please."

She poured him a glass and then brought her plate around to his side of the counter and sat down next to him.

He realized he wasn't interested in food. He'd forgotten what it was like to have a woman in his home. To have a woman take care of him.

"Mrs. Ranney said that strawberry-rhubarb was your favorite."

"It used to be."

"Do you want me to get you something else?" she asked.

"Yes."

She started to hop off her stool, and he lifted her up and settled her on his lap. "What are you doing?"

"Having something sweet."

"I didn't realize I was sweet."

"You're tongue is sharp, but your kisses, *ma petite,* they are very sweet."

"So are yours," she said. She wrapped her arms around his shoulders and held him close. "I missed you tonight. Your apartment is so big. I felt very lonely without you."

Lonely. That was a word he'd learned to ignore for a long time.

He thought about the future, and for the first time he realized he was *looking* at the future. One that he wanted with Sheri. Not as his wife, because he'd already given his name to the one woman who'd owned his heart.

But he did want her to stay with him. Wanted Sheri to be in his life, and not just at work.

"You're staring at me," she said. "Why?"

"Because I like the way you look at me."

"Ah, ego. I should have known."

He just shook his head. Then kissed her one more time, because he couldn't resist her mouth when it was this close.

He lifted her in his arms and carried her down the hall to his bedroom. Laying her in the center of his bed, he came down over her, bracing his weight on his forearms so that there was a small gap between their bodies.

"I want you to live with me."

"I am living with you," she said.

"I mean, even after the engagement party and my family goes home."

"Am I here for them?" she asked.

"No, *ma petite*. You are here for me, and I'm asking you to stay."

Sheri held her breath as Tristan lowered himself over her. She would never say it out loud, but she loved the feel of him on top of her. It made their relationship real when, after they made love, she'd wrap her arms and legs around him and just hold him, pretending she never had to let go.

But now, she thought, she might not have to let go. She didn't know what he meant by asking her to stay, but it sounded positive. She couldn't believe she'd waited so long to move in with him. Granted it had only been for a little over a week. But their lives had meshed together.

She liked living with him. For the first time in her entire life, she felt like she was in the place where she was meant to be with the man to whom she belonged.

"What do you mean?"

"That I want you to stay with me, and not just as my temporary fiancée. I want this to be permanent."

She felt a rush of joy and she tipped her head back, blinking so he wouldn't see the tears in her eyes. She took a deep breath and felt the gentle stroking of his finger against the side of her cheek.

"So what do you think?"

Her gaze met his and she tried to read the emotions there, but as always she had no idea what he was feeling. But she knew what *she* felt. She loved this man. She wanted nothing more than to say she was his and live the rest of her life with him.

"I think yes. I'd love to spend the rest of my life with you."

He gave her a tight smile and kissed her. "Great."

"Great? That's all you can say?"

"It seemed more appropriate than 'get naked.'"

She laughed and hugged him tightly to her. "Get naked would work."

"Really?"

"Yes!"

He laughed then, and she felt a sense of rightness deep down in her soul. In that empty part that had been hollow since her father had left all those long years ago.

He started to unbutton her blouse and she put her hands in his thick hair, rubbing the back of his scalp as he undressed her. She thought of the wedding plans she'd put off making, because planning a wedding she wasn't going to follow through with had seemed like torture. But now she could stop putting off Blanche and really start thinking about the kind of bride she'd be.

"When do you want to get married? I know we'd been putting off picking a date because of the pretense, but now that we're going through with it things are different."

Tristan stopped unbuttoning her blouse and lifted himself off of her body. "Married?"

"Isn't that what you meant, Tristan? If we're going to live together permanently..."

He pushed completely off her and sat on the edge of the bed, his back to her. And she realized he hadn't meant marriage. "What were you thinking?"

"That we'd live together," he answered.

"What's the difference in living together and being married?" she asked. "Everyone already thinks we're engaged."

"I don't give a damn what everyone thinks. We both know that we aren't really engaged," he said, glancing over his shoulder at her.

She shook her head, fiddling with the ring he'd given her, and realized that her shirt was unbuttoned and she was still laying in the middle of his bed. She sat up and quickly refastened her shirt.

"I don't know what to think anymore," she said, climbing off the king-size bed. "I never know what to expect from you, Tristan."

"I do not understand," he said.

And for the first time, she realized that he really didn't understand what she was talking about. Because Tristan was always looking out for himself. For his own desires, his own safety. She had been thinking that because he showered her with attention and gifts, he was caring for her.

"I love you. Do you remember that?"

He stood up and walked over to her. He touched her so softly, tracing the lines of her face with his fingertip. "I do remember it. Hearing you say you love me is something that I think about a lot."

"And…?"

"And that's why I want us to continue living together."

She staggered back away from him. "Did you ask me because you feel sorry for me?"

He shook his head. "I asked because I'm tired

of being alone. And you bring something to my life that I never thought to find again."

"Love," she said. "I bring love to your life."

"No, you bring that to yourself. To me you bring companionship and friendship…an end to the loneliness I've felt when I'm around other couples."

She didn't know what to say. Because she had the feeling that he'd asked her to live with him out of pity. She realized for the first time that her father had done her a huge favor by leaving. Because Tristan staying with her out of guilt or pity made her feel worse than being left behind.

"What are you going to do?" Tristan asked Sheri. He could tell that things weren't going the way he wanted them to. If there were a way for him to go back ten minutes, he would have kept his mouth shut.

"I don't know what I'm going to do. Obviously I gave you my word that I'd stay with you until the party and that's…in two days, right? So after the party I'll move back to the brownstone."

He knew he shouldn't be mad at Sheri. But he was. If she wasn't so stuck in her bourgeois American idea of what a relationship should be, then he'd have everything he wanted. "Running back to your favorite hiding place?"

"I'm not running," she said, crossing her arms around her waist and staring up at him with those big wounded doe eyes.

But this time he didn't let the eyes affect him. He knew better. She was as manipulative as the other women he'd dated. The ones that had always wanted to be Mrs. Tristan Sabina and had schemed to get there. Sheri was the same, she just went about it differently. "It sure seems that way from where I'm standing. You said you loved me, and now that I won't marry you…you're going back to the same place you've always run to."

She dropped her arms and stalked over to him. "Well, you'd know all about running. Of course, you hide out in the public eye. Dating a bunch of different shallow women. Acting like nothing in life affects you."

Tristan couldn't argue with that. "What do you want from me?"

"I don't know."

"Don't hedge, Sheri. Tell me what you want. How can I make this right for you?"

She turned away and then glanced back at him. "You could love me."

He didn't know how to answer that. "I'm...I can't do that."

She nodded. "Then you have nothing I want."

She walked to the bedroom door and he realized that she was leaving. That she was going to walk out that door and he wasn't ready for her to go.

"Sheri."

"Yes?"

"I really want you to stay."

She looked back at him. "I want to. But for the first time in my life, I realize that I can't keep settling for the least bit of attention. You changed me over the last few weeks. Made me into a different woman. And the one constant through all of that is how much I love you.

"But tonight, I realized that loving you isn't enough for me, and it's not fair to you. You need something more. Something I can't give."

He didn't know what she was talking about, but could tell that it made a lot of sense to Sheri. "Are you leaving tonight?"

"No. I gave you my word I'd stay through our pretend engagement party."

"Very well. Thank you for that," he said, gathering his facade around him. He always knew how to put on a good face. And it wasn't like he really loved her. She was his *pretend* fiancée. "I'll sleep down the hall."

"Okay."

He walked out of his bedroom. In the wide, long hallway he heard her footsteps behind him. "Tristan."

He looked back.

"I thought you were different," she said, her voice sad and low but still audible.

"Different how?"

"I don't know, just different from the other men in my life."

"I am sure I am different."

"On the outside you are very different. But inside, you're the same."

"Same how?"

"Hollow and empty. Unwilling to let your guard down for a second and accept the gift of my love."

Her words were heartfelt, and to be honest, he did feel an ache deep inside at her words. He'd thought for a long time that he wasn't exactly the man he used to be.

"I have a full life. After you break our engagement I will be back to my busy schedule and the life that I have become accustomed to."

"That doesn't mean that you're happy."

He saw the tears in her wide brown eyes and

knew he was going to remember that look on her face for a long time.

"Happiness is a fool's notion."

"No, it's not. Unless you think it's foolish to take a risk. To put yourself on the line. And I know you don't, because you take risks every day in business. At the Sabina Group, and with the nightclubs you own with Gui and Christos. It's only in your personal life that you refuse to take a chance."

He pivoted on his heel and walked back to her. "Studying me in magazines and tabloid stories does not mean you know who I am and what makes me tick."

"No, it doesn't," she said. "What makes me an expert is having fallen in love with you. And living with you this week has shown me a man that few people really see. I do know the real you."

"Do you? Who is the real me?"

She took a deep breath and looked up at him. In her bare feet, he felt like he towered over her. "The real you. Are you sure you want to know?"

"I asked, did I not?"

"That's right. You did. Well, the real man I've seen, Tristan, is a coward. Someone who's felt a deep pain, and I'm not discounting that. But because of one loss, you've cut yourself off from ever loving again. And that seems cowardly to me."

Tristan didn't answer her, just walked away. And this time he wasn't coming back. He wasn't a coward, and he wasn't about to let Sheri Donnelly use those words to make him do something he knew he'd regret.

Twelve

Sheri left early and arrived at the office before Tristan. He called from the limo and asked her to join him going to the airport to pick up his family. She made an excuse about being too busy, and he let it go.

She knew she would have to see him again tomorrow night at their engagement gala, but until then she was hiding out. She had never had a broken heart before. She wished she could fall out of love with Tristan, but it simply wasn't that easy.

He'd been the embodiment of every romantic

fantasy she'd ever had. The lover she'd always wanted. He'd made her feel as if she was the sexiest woman alive, and the pleasure he'd evoked in her body was beyond even her wildest fantasies. And the way he'd taken care of her… The way she'd felt when she was with him…

Working and living with Tristan had made her believe she'd found the other half of her soul. That she'd brought things to his life that had been lacking, and he'd done the same for her.

She put her head on her desk and realized that she wasn't going to be able to stay on here at the Sabina Group. There was no way she could sit in this office every day and pretend that she wasn't still in love with Tristan.

It was well after six and she was still working. She was scheduled to meet Tristan and his family and friends at Del Posto for dinner at eight-thirty. After calling Tristan a coward, she couldn't stand him up.

Her phone rang.

"Sabina Group, this is Sheri."

"Sheri, this is Palmer at the security desk. There is a Count Guillermo de Cuaron y Bautista de la Cruz here to see you."

"To see *me?*"

"Yes."

Why was Gui here? "Please send him up."

"I will."

She hung up the phone and pulled her mirror out of the bottom drawer of her desk, thinking she should fix her makeup, then realized she hadn't put any on this morning. She'd reverted to the old Sheri. She needed the comfort of her big comfy clothes and her plain appearance. There was a lot to be said for not being noticed.

"Ms. Donnelly, I'd like a word with you." Gui strode into her office like he owned it. But he stopped in his path and put his hands on his hips, cursing succinctly under his breath. She caught about every other word, since his Spanish accent was fairly heavy. "What the hell is going on with you and Tristan?"

"I think you should ask him that question. I'm taking care of some last-minute things here at the office. I think we're all meeting at the restaurant for dinner."

He shook his head. "I already talked to him, at the airport. And I came over here to find out what has happened between the two of you."

"Ask him again."

"I thought the problem was you."

She glanced up at Gui and realized there was a bit of truth in what he'd said. "The problem *is* me."

Gui shook his head. "How is it you?"

"I want things from him that he can't give me."

"Love?"

"How'd you know?"

"Because I know Tristan, and that's the one thing he thinks he cannot offer you."

There was something about Gui that made her want to pour out her soul. Something so understanding in those hazel eyes of his. "I think it might be me. I'm not the kind of woman who inspires that in any man."

"Don't say that, Sheri. Tristan wasn't always the man you see before you today."

"He wasn't?"

"He was badly hurt when Cecile died. He used to be the most gregarious of all of us. So filled with a big joy for loving. And then when Cecile was diagnosed with cancer…he thought they'd beat it at first. He put his entire life on hold to stay by her side."

Sheri ached to hear his words, but they mirrored what she already knew. Tristan had told her himself that he couldn't love anymore. That he'd had his once in a lifetime. It was just her bad luck that she had found *her* forever-love in him.

"I know all that. I thought I could love him enough for both of us. But that was silly, and now we're both moving on."

"I'm not sure that you haven't changed him, Sheri. He's a different man today than he was at Christos's wedding, and that's thanks to you."

"I doubt that. I'm not the type of woman who can change a man's life."

Gui sat down on the corner of her desk. "Yes, you are. Don't give up on him yet. Will you give him one more chance?"

She shook her head. She couldn't bear the pain of losing him again.

The phone rang, but it was after hours so she let it go to voice mail. "Why do you care?"

"Because Tristan is one of my dearest friends and you've made him happier in the last few weeks than I've seen him in years."

She was afraid to believe him. But at the same time, she knew Gui wouldn't lie to her. "I'm afraid to take another chance on him. I just made up my mind that he wasn't going to stay with me."

"You strike me as a fighter, Sheri. Someone who wouldn't let the chance of a lifetime slip away."

She looked up at Gui and realized that he was right. She was letting go of Tristan too easily. She loved the man, and that wasn't going to change. Shouldn't she keep fighting for him?

Sheri's absence was palpable to Tristan as the day drew on. Blanche and Rene had a lot of questions about her, and the more he talked with his siblings about her, the more he realized how much he cared for her.

When they got back to his place, he waited for Sheri to come and greet them but she must still be at the office, hiding from him. He felt the emptiness in a new way. Echoing around him.

Gui had been shocked by how he looked. When Tristan had mentioned that the engagement was definitely off, Gui had left in disgust to run an errand. And Tristan realized that his plan to make Sheri his fake fiancée hadn't been well thought out. He'd never considered how he'd feel when she left his life.

Blanche had nothing but good things to say about Sheri and Tristan found himself laughing at the stories she told about shopping with the woman he'd been trying to keep out of his heart for the last few weeks. As he pictured her in his mind, he realized he hadn't done a very good job of it.

He loved her. How could he not have realized

what he was feeling for her? The only excuse he had was that it was different than the sweet and gentle love he'd had for his Cecile. With Sheri the love was bigger than he was, passionate. And that's what had him running scared.

Dammit, she had been right when she'd called him a coward. He had been running from her, because he'd been afraid to risk being hurt again.

Realizing that, he knew he had to make things right for her. Had to find a way to win her back before she had to face his friends and family tomorrow night at the engagement gala. He wanted it to be a real celebration, otherwise what was the point?

He called the office, but Sheri's phone went to voice mail. He hung up without leaving a message. He had no idea when she was going to show up, or even where she was. But he did know she'd come to the restaurant for dinner. Because she always kept her word.

And that was another reason he loved her. She wasn't fickle or shallow. She couldn't tell a lie to him. Her love would never leave him, or let him feel betrayed.

He knew he needed to do something to show Sheri that he was serious about her and that he wasn't running away any longer. And he knew it would take more than the hour he had until he was supposed to start meeting his friends and family at Del Posto. He went and found his mother.

"Maman?"

"*Oui*, Tristan."

"I need your help."

"With?"

"I've hurt the woman I love and I need to make a big gesture to make it up to her, but we have reservations at a restaurant across town."

"How can I help, *mon fils?*"

"Be my hostess while I take care of a few details here. And when Sheri arrives, keep her there."

"Where will you be?"

"Taking care of details," he said, kissing his mother on the forehead.

"Okay, I'll do this. Are you sure about this girl? You always swore love was no longer in the cards for you."

"*Oui, maman.* I am more than sure. She's reawakened a part of me I thought was dead."

His mother smiled at him and then hugged him tightly. "I'm so glad to hear it. A part of me has long wept for that deadness inside you."

After his family left for the restaurant, Tristan made several quick, demanding phone calls.

Knowing the kind of romantic person Sheri was, with her secret dreams of how love should be, he arranged for flowers to fill the apartment. He ordered the finest French champagne sent up from his wine cellar and then called his favorite jeweler for a necklace. When the flowers arrived, he decked out the balcony to resemble the one at his villa that night in Mykonos. Now he had every detail he could think of in place—except for Sheri.

His mobile rang. A quick glance at the caller ID window showed him it was Gui. "What's up, Gui?"

"Where are you?"

"My place. Why?"

"Because Sheri is at the restaurant turning heads, but she's asking where you are. You need to get down here."

"I'm on my way. Don't let her leave."

"I won't."

Tristan's driver had him across town in no time at all. He walked into the restaurant and stopped in his tracks. Sheri wasn't sitting quietly in a corner the way she had during many of the activities that week back on Mykonos. Instead, she was in the center of his family and friends, wearing a stylish dress and holding court. He couldn't move as his heart skipped a beat.

This was what he'd been afraid to let himself see. That Sheri was the other half of his soul and he needed her more than he'd ever expected to need any woman. If she left him... God, he couldn't even go there in hypothetical. He needed her.

How could he have thought he'd be able to survive without her in his life?

He walked up to her and all the words he'd rehearsed escaped him. He saw her flush as he looked at her. He wanted her and he was sure she knew the signs of his arousal well enough by now to tell that. But he wanted more than just her sexy little body. He also wanted the joy in her eyes, the witty, sassy mouth of hers. He wanted it all.

And he didn't want to tell her in front of the world. She deserved to hear about how he felt for her the first time in private. Where he could do a proper job of it.

"Tristan?"

"Hmm?"

"Are you okay?"

He shook his head. "I'm tired."

"Well, I'm sorry to hear that," she said.

"Don't you want to know why?"

She nibbled on her lower lip. "Okay, I'll ask. Why are you tired?"

"Because I've been running for too long."

"What have you been running from?"

"I've been running from you, *ma petite,* and that has to stop." He reached out and snagged her wrist. "Please excuse us," he said to his family.

"Not so fast. We want to hear more about this running you've been doing."

"Forget it, Rene. My private life is supposed to be private. Isn't that what you've been telling me?"

"Indeed," Rene said.

Christos and Ava stepped in between Rene and Tristan to say hello. They looked wonderful together, smiling and happy and…loving. Tristan clapped his hand on his friend's shoulder, thanking him for flying in and promising to see them the next day. Then he drew Sheri away from the crowd and toward the exit.

"Why are we leaving? You just arrived."

"I need to be alone with you."

Tristan didn't say much in the car ride from Del Posto to his apartment, but he held her hand the entire time, rubbing his thumb against her palm and bringing her hand to his mouth several times to kiss it.

She wondered if simply changing her attitude

had changed his, but she knew that couldn't be it. Something had happened to Tristan, too. He was acting so different. When they got to his apartment building, he held her hand all the way up in the elevator and then made her close her eyes when they got to the front door.

"Why?"

"Because I said so."

"And I'm going to do this why?" she asked, teasing him.

He lifted her off her feet and into his arms, kissing her hard. "Stop sassing me or I really will spank you."

She shook her head. "Tristan, what is going on with you?"

"I am in love."

Tears burned her eyes as those words came from his mouth. She didn't believe them. He'd been too adamant about not falling again. "Put me down."

"No."

"Tristan, I mean it."

"So do I."

He reached down, unlocked his front door and carried her over the threshold. He set her on her feet in the foyer. She was blinking, trying not to cry, but it wasn't working.

"I wanted to do this properly."

"Do what properly? You don't have to pretend to feel something for me you don't feel."

"I am not pretending, *ma petite*."

She wasn't sure she believed him, but she knew he wouldn't lie to her. He never had.

"When did you realize you loved me?" she asked him.

"Today, when I was surrounded by my family. I did not realize how much you'd done with them. They were all telling me stories about you and I realized that no matter how hard I'd tried not to fall for you, I already had.

"I love you, Sheri. And it does scare me. Because as much as I thought that Cecile was my once-in-a-lifetime love, I have come to realize that love is also what I feel for you. I need you in my life."

She was afraid to believe him. "It's okay if you don't love me. I'm not going to walk away from you like I did last night. That was wrong—"

"You are not listening to me, *ma petite*. I love you. I am not going anywhere without you anymore. No running unless you are by my side."

She was still afraid to believe him but there was sincerity in his eyes that made her want to.

He must have read the hesitation on her face

because he leaned down and kissed her. And when he lifted his head he said, softly, "I am not going anywhere."

Those words she believed. No man had ever said them to her before. "Promise?"

"Yes, I do. What about you?"

"I'm not going anywhere, either. I'm staying by your side from now on."

"Why is that?"

"I love you, Tristan."

He smiled at her and lifted her off her feet. He carried her through his apartment out onto the balcony that offered a splendid view of the Manhattan skyline.

"You're already wearing my engagement ring, but I need to ask you again…Sheri Donnelly, my love, the woman who owns my heart, will you marry me?"

She looked up at him as he stood next to her on the balcony. Taking a deep breath, she leaned up and kissed him before pulling back. "Yes, Tristan, I will marry you."

He pulled her into his arms and made love to her, sealing the bond they'd just made with their bodies. And she knew she'd found the happiness she'd always thought would elude her. She and

Tristan had found something rare, the kind of love that touched few people's lives, and she felt blessed to have him as her own.

* * * * *

Wealth and power are nothing without love!
Don't miss Gui's story next month as
Katherine Garbera's SONS OF PRIVILEGE
miniseries continues with
THE SPANISH ARISTOCRAT'S WOMAN.
Available in March 2008.
Only from Silhouette Desire!

Silhouette®

Desire

Buy 2 Silhouette Desire books and receive

$1.⁰⁰ off

your purchase of the ~~Silhouette Desire novel~~
Iron Cowboy by *New York Times* bestselling author

DIANA PALMER

on sale March 2008.

Receive $1.⁰⁰ off

**the Silhouette Desire novel IRON COWBOY,
on sale March 2008, when you purchase
2 Silhouette Desire books.**

*Available wherever books are sold including most bookstores,
supermarkets, drugstores and discount stores.*

Coupon expires August 31, 2008. Redeemable at participating retail
outlets in the U.S. only. Limit one coupon per customer.

RETAILERS: Harlequin Enterprises Limited will pay the face value of this coupon plus 8¢ if
submitted by the customer for this specified product only. Any other use constitutes fraud.
Coupon is nonassignable. Void if taxed, prohibited or restricted by law. Consumer must pay
any government taxes. Void if copied. For reimbursement submit coupons and proof of sales
directly to Harlequin Enterprises Limited, P.O. Box 880478, El Paso, TX 88588-0478, U.S.A.
Cash value 1/100 cents. Limit one coupon per customer. Valid in the U.S. only.

11470

5 65373 00076 2   (8100)0 11470

SDCPNUS0208

Silhouette Desire

Buy 2 Silhouette Desire books and receive

$1.⁰⁰ off

your purchase of the Silhouette Desire novel
Iron Cowboy by *New York Times* bestselling author

DIANA PALMER

on sale March 2008.

Receive $1.⁰⁰ off

**the Silhouette Desire novel IRON COWBOY,
on sale March 2008, when you purchase
2 Silhouette Desire books.**

*Available wherever books are sold including most bookstores,
supermarkets, drugstores and discount stores.*

Coupon expires August 31, 2008. Redeemable at participating retail
outlets in Canada only. Limit one coupon per customer.

52608214

SDCPNCAN0208

REQUEST YOUR FREE BOOKS!

2 FREE NOVELS PLUS 2 FREE GIFTS!

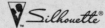

Passionate, Powerful, Provocative!

YES! Please send me 2 FREE Silhouette Desire® novels and my 2 FREE gifts. After receiving them, if I don't wish to receive any more books, I can return the shipping statement marked "cancel." If I don't cancel, I will receive 6 brand-new novels every month and be billed just $3.80 per book in the U.S., or $4.47 per book in Canada, plus 25¢ shipping and handling per book and applicable taxes, if any*. That's a savings of almost 15% off the cover price! I understand that accepting the 2 free books and gifts places me under no obligation to buy anything. I can always return a shipment and cancel at any time. Even if I never buy another book from Silhouette, the two free books and gifts are mine to keep forever.

225 SDN EEXJ 326 SDN EEXU

Name _____ (PLEASE PRINT)

Address _____ Apt. _____

City _____ State/Prov. _____ Zip/Postal Code _____

Signature (if under 18, a parent or guardian must sign)

Mail to the **Silhouette Reader Service™:**
IN U.S.A.: P.O. Box 1867, Buffalo, NY 14240-1867
IN CANADA: P.O. Box 609, Fort Erie, Ontario L2A 5X3

Not valid to current Silhouette Desire subscribers.

Want to try two free books from another line?
Call 1-800-873-8635 or visit www.morefreebooks.com.

* Terms and prices subject to change without notice. NY residents add applicable sales tax. Canadian residents will be charged applicable provincial taxes and GST. This offer is limited to one order per household. All orders subject to approval. Credit or debit balances in a customer's account(s) may be offset by any other outstanding balance owed by or to the customer. Please allow 4 to 6 weeks for delivery.

Your Privacy: Silhouette is committed to protecting your privacy. Our Privacy Policy is available online at www.eHarlequin.com or upon request from the Reader Service. From time to time we make our lists of customers available to reputable firms who may have a product or service of interest to you. If you would prefer we not share your name and address, please check here. ☐

SDES07

COMING NEXT MONTH

#1855 MISTRESS & A MILLION DOLLARS—
Maxine Sullivan
Diamonds Down Under
He will stop at nothing to get what he wants. And if it costs him a million dollars to make her his mistress...so be it!

#1856 IRON COWBOY—Diana Palmer
Long, Tall Texans
He was as ornery as they come. But this billionaire Texan didn't stand a chance of escaping the one woman who was his match...in every way.

#1857 BARGAINING FOR KING'S BABY—Maureen Child
Kings of California
He agreed to marry his rival's daughter to settle a business deal...but she has her own bargain for her soon-to-be husband. Give her a baby or lose the contract!

#1858 THE SPANISH ARISTOCRAT'S WOMAN—
Katherine Garbera
Sons of Privilege
She was only supposed to play the count's lover for one day. But suddenly, she's become his wife.

#1859 CEO'S MARRIAGE SEDUCTION—Anna DePalo
It was the perfect plan. Wed her father's business protégé and have the baby she's been dreaming about...until scandals threaten her plan for the perfect marriage of convenience.

#1860 FOR BLACKMAIL...OR PLEASURE—Robyn Grady
Blackmailing his ex-fiancée into working for him was easy. Denying the attraction still between them could prove to be lethal.